JUDY SANDRA

THE METAL GIRL

 JSM Books

ISBN: 978-0-578-03878-0

PRINTED IN THE UNITED STATES OF AMERICA

To the memory of Ursule Molinaro

"Fortunately analysis is not the only way to resolve inner conflicts. Life itself still remains a very effective therapist."

Karen Horney, *Our Inner Conflicts*

Chapter 1

The first time I drank beer in Denmark, I nearly passed out. In Denmark beer has the alcoholic content of wine in America and no one told me, not even my guidebook, *Europe on No Dollars a Day*, whose advice I was trying to follow so ardently that trip, my first–my only–trip to Europe.

I was sitting in the Royal Café, a pub below street level, recommended by the book, of course, as being the "in" place, near the opera house, frequented by the intelligentsia of Copenhagen. Now, in mid-March, in the late afternoon, I was surrounded by a roomful of Danish businessmen getting sloshed after work. It was the happy hour. I was not happy; I was bored and lonely. Why else would I have been sitting in that pretentious café in a foreign city all alone, drinking Tuborg beer, which nobody warned me was as strong as wine? I felt ridiculously stupid drinking beer by myself, nervous and conspicuous. I did not notice any Danish women sitting by themselves at small tables like me.

I drank the entire bottle in a matter of minutes. Then, as if someone had turned the engine of my carousel up to full speed, the room began to spin. I couldn't make it stop, and I couldn't move because, if I did, I'd either throw up or faint. I sat very still, closed my eyes and lowered my head, hoping beyond hope that no one noticed. With my elbows on the table, I held my head in my hands until the dizziness went away and the hanging brass lamps, the rows of wineglasses suspended from the ceiling rack, the clubby men leaning against the bar, and their reflections in the bar mirror stood still again.

If I had been smart I would have left, cleared my head with the cold air and caught the remaining light of day. But I wasn't smart in those days, at least not smart enough, and as soon as I perked up, I ordered another Tuborg. This time I sipped it very slowly, like drinking wine. I was in no hurry. I had nowhere in particular to go, nothing special planned for that evening. And, to be truthful, I would have welcomed a glance of recognition, a hello, a may-I-sit-here, a date, a sexual adventure from one of these unescorted men, that is, one not so squarely business-suited. I had my limits.

So there I sat, the young American woman, attractively dressed, sweetly perfumed, available, free, a comely little fish in a little Danish pond. Only no other fish swam my way. I had to admit, as a siren, I was an undeniable failure.

Finally, my empty bottle prompted me to leave. I had

had enough beer and enough also of this "charming" dark, smoky pub. I surfaced into the old streets again and the winter sunset over the city.

Copenhagen is not as snowy and cold in March as it is damp and gray, and I still wonder why I went to Europe at all that winter, my 25th winter. At the time I merely asked myself, "Why not?" I was unemployed, unable to decide between my short-lived career in academic public relations or trying something new; in the dumps from yet another broken off, very brief and not very meaningful love affair; and living in a small, drab New England city that hibernated in the grim winter and, at best, lolled against a polluted river in summer.

I was down, far down. The only way to go was up, up in the air, on the Scandinavian airlines, with their low winter fares, up and over the ocean and down onto this quaint little city of islands in this odd, distant country.

My friends, excited for me, had whisked me off to the airport, littered me with token travel gifts, and toasted me in a jolly bon voyage send-off in the airport lounge. Even as I waved good-bye to them from the jetway and took off in the large, empty plane, I had no real idea what I was doing or what lay ahead of me in that blue beyond. All I knew was that I was uplifting myself, I was asserting my independence, I was becoming a Woman-of-the-World (whatever that meant). And I was going to a new, a far corner of the world to do so.

Perhaps it was those outdated expressions that got me

into trouble. This was the early 1970's, the era of heightened feminist consciousness. But my mind had not yet caught up to my age, and my consciousness was not the part of me that was rising up that winter.

The fading yellow light bounced off the old yellow buildings as I made my way back to the Hotel Blumendahl. It was not a great distance from the café. Nothing in Copenhagen is a great distance from one point to another in the main part of the city, which is remarkably small. I easily navigated the winding but well-marked streets and rarely took public transportation; there was much to see within walking distance.

The route back to the hotel first took me through narrow residential streets. Every once in a while I discovered thin alleyways between ancient buildings made of old brick and stone. I followed the alleys to secret, medieval-looking and mysteriously unoccupied inner courtyards, which I couldn't help exploring. Next I passed through a shopping area of streets designed solely for pedestrians, the Strøget. There were exclusive shops that sold modern Danish crafts and less expensive gift shops, clothing stores, and tourist shops with traditional hand-knit sweaters and woolens. The shops that particularly caught my attention were the sex shops.

Except for the very posh streets, the sex shops prevailed unabashedly everywhere, sandwiched between the most innocuous establishments, coexisting beside a shoe store or a jewelry store or a coffee shop. The sex shops mushroomed over the city in such enormous numbers, one could hardly miss them. Their signs were always written in English and said "Sex Shop," in big bold capitals, with no attempt to hide their purpose. They did not sell sex, as one might wonder. They sold pornography and, I suppose, sex paraphernalia. I never ventured inside these small shops. I was wary of them, and I wasn't in the market for sexual exotica. Although if sex itself had been a commodity on the shelf, I might have considered the merchandise, or at least have browsed.

I wondered how so many sex shops in one small city could thrive. Whenever I posed this question to the Danes they insisted that the "shops" served the tourists. I doubted this. In mid-March cold, rainy, gray Copenhagen attracts few tourists from any direction, and I had paid close enough attention to the shops to notice how they seemed busy all the time—even late at night.

The day continued to unfold.

I soon turned off the wide main avenue and followed the secondary road to my hotel at the edge of the city center. It was a quiet residential area with clean, flat streets of low limestone and brick row houses and, though obviously not one of the better districts of the city, far from what one would consider the worst in America. I assumed it was a working class neighborhood, though I rarely saw my neighbors. My hotel was not really a hotel either, in the usual sense. It was more like a boarding house, which occupied the third floor of a five-story apartment building, with a metal HOTEL sign hanging outside its third-floor window. It housed transients like me as well as permanent boarders.

This street was always quite deserted. Hardly a car passed. Even now, in the early evening, I saw no one for many blocks, walking by the dark apartment houses and small stores, closing up for the night.

I had learned to walk on the sidewalk and never to drift into the bicycle lane, after one encounter with an irate cyclist speeding on a heavy, fat-wheeled bicycle. I bounced along now. The cold air had sobered me and, after all, I was having an exciting European vacation.

I walked easily on the very flat, very straight street and soon drifted into a mindless reverie, lost in a touristy mood, observing insignificant yet eye-catching details, like the foreign names and lettering on the street signs. I stopped at one corner, trying to decipher a sign with a name I couldn't fathom how to pronounce, much as I tried. Giving up, I stepped off the curb to cross the street when a small hand gripped my left shoulder and pulled me back and a loud, belligerent female voice assaulted my left ear.

I instinctively yanked myself free and spun around. I faced a tiny elderly woman, who yelled at me in Danish while pointing to the red traffic light, which was glowing red and revealed the white outline of a man with an X across his body. The woman's face also turned red as she continued berating me in Danish and violently miming with her hands the act of a policeman writing a ticket, in other words warning me, that I would get a ticket for jay-walking. There she was, trying to save me from this imminent and despicable fate.

"Oh," I said and nodded my head in that internationally understood up and down gesture, "thank you," feeling anything but thankful.

For one thing she had scared me, grabbing me from behind like that. Then I felt chastised, as if I had been caught committing a sin. I was embarrassed to be accused of an uncivic transgression in public, like a naive child ignorant of the social rules, yet who, nonetheless, has just had her hand slapped. And there stood *I*, foreigner, adventuress, Woman-of-the-World, waiting with this matriarch at a traffic-less corner for the light to change so that I wouldn't get a ticket for jay-walking from a non-existent policeman.

The instant the light changed I sped across the street, hurrying the rest of the way, soon out-distancing the authoritarian woman and arriving at the Hotel Blumendahl before I knew it.

I inserted the key and unlocked the front door. That was quaint. I needed a key to enter the apartment building, like any other tenant on the two floors below or the two above. Turning the key in the lock gave me a sense of home, of belonging here. Then I faced the winding dark wood staircase snaking around the small central elevator, the closed apartment doors with their owners' names engraved on bold brass plaques, the cotton candy pink plaster walls, and was reminded of being far from home in every sense.

Mr. Blumendahl sat at the desk, absorbed in his book-keeping. When he saw me approach the glass door of the hotel, which opened to the hall across from the elevator, he leapt up and opened it for me, smiling and giving me an avuncular "hello" as I glided past him.

The Blumendahls both treated me sweetly, and I'm sure they were appreciative of my proposed two-week booking. In these first few days, I had already proven myself a quiet, reliable and responsible guest. They obviously needed the business; many rooms remained uninhabited, and the only regular boarders were the two middle-aged bachelors who lived at the end of the long dimly lit corridor.

Mr. Blumendahl was a stocky man with a receding hairline and luminous brown eyes that blinked often and smiled quizzically. He wore a uniform-like outfit of maroon and navy sweater vests and baggy trousers but was very neat and clean, down to his immaculately manicured fingernails. Mrs. Blumendahl was also dark, short and chubby. They matched each other like a set of hand-painted ceramic salt-and-pepper shakers, the antique kind one finds in thrift shops. She had a round face with dumpling cheeks, liquid brown eyes, a warm smile. She too wore a uniform: either a two-piece wool knit blouse and skirt or a shapeless house dress, quite out-of-date but what one would expect of an aging European matron. She twisted her graying brown hair into a tight chignon on top of her head. She never wore slacks or anything casual, never let her hair fall loosely down her back. She was an old-fashioned Woman–girdled, bound, coiffed, and chastely clothed.

Theirs was a traditional arrangement: Mr. Blumendahl managed the bookings and the finances. Mrs. Blumendahl cleaned the rooms, washed the linens and prepared and served the meager though tasty complimentary continental breakfast. Watching Mrs. Blumendahl waddle down the hall with a stack of sheets and towels was a comforting sight. I felt taken care of, a guest in the home of a kindly aunt and uncle, not a traveler in a cheap, foreign hotel. I could forget the cold linoleum floors, the shared bathroom down the hall, the kitschy faded reproductions on the walls, and my solitary room with worn, uncomfortable metal furniture to sit and sleep on, and one lone window with a view only of another apartment building across the alley.

I anticipated this view as I returned Mr. Blumendahl's "hello" and smiled and nodded my head, while he closed the door behind me. Which was the extent of our exchanges. Mr. Blumendahl's English was minimal and, therefore, conversation was brief. I certainly didn't speak Danish nor did I know the Blumenndahl's native language or where they were from. I had assumed, being Jewish in Denmark, they must be refugees from the WAR. This made them even more dramatic and romantic to me. The War. Refugees. Words of Europe, of unknown lands. There it was before me–The Danish Underground, Intrigue, Life and Death escapades.

"Thank you," I said, acknowledging Mr. Blumendahl's chivalry, nodded again, and fluttered down the hallway to my room.

As I closed the door behind me and turned on the lamp beside the bed, I was not thinking about refugees. I was thinking that the beer had given me a headache, and I was hungry. I hung my damp coat on a plain wire hanger, slightly bowed on the bottom edge, in the old and very small mahogany wardrobe, which served as a closet. I took two aspirin with water in the clean glass provided for me every day on the narrow shelf above the sink. The small white porcelain sink stuck out from the wall like a goiter on someone's otherwise smooth neck, an unhealthy aberration in a room of four otherwise flat walls.

My travel toothbrush hung neatly on a toothbrush rack. I saw it there, an ordinary chrome rack, an ordinary toothbrush. An ordinary sink, an ordinary slab of mirror stuck to the wall, an ordinary face staring out of it.

The glass made a dull "clink" when I replaced it on the shelf. I sat at the foot of my bed and stared at my weary feet. I flicked off my walking shoes with my toes and lay back on the bed. I looked straight up, at the white ceiling, its mute whiteness like a large, blank canvas. Closing my eyes, I wished, oh wished, there was someone else in that bed with me.

Then there was. A dark faceless figure, whom I sensed more than saw. I couldn't see the exact shape or hair color. What difference had that ever made? Only sensations mattered. The sweet smell of skin. The touch. A tingling started at my breasts and traveled downward. I felt gentle hands caressing me. But alas, they were my own.

My dress rose up, my underwear fell down. I lay there, my eyes shut, my "friend" present. I touched myself and rose, to a place beyond time, space, and continental borders.

I had dozed off. When I came to, my flesh was cold. I wrapped myself in a bathrobe and noticed that the curtains had been open, with the light on. Someone could have seen me...The very thought was embarrassing.

Now, at the window, I clutched my robe at the neck and boldly looked out at the lit windows in the apartment building across the alley made of a chalky gray stone. Wondering...but, no. Most everyone's blinds, curtains, shades were closed for the evening, bright lights shining from within, except for one brazenly exposed window, ablaze with light, which now seemed so daring compared to the other shuttered rooms.

It was a dining room. A woman was setting a table for two. I could clearly see her arranging plates, silverware, glasses and cloth napkins on the table. This scene fascinated me, and I couldn't stop watching her, perhaps because my stomach was growling and a homemade meal on a familiar table looked so inviting.

A man entered, placed an opened bottle of wine on the table and sat down. The woman left and came back with the food. He poured the wine. I watched them eat, the couple, their life framed by that rectangular window, as if by a camera's eye. Theirs was an ordinary life, which I watched for a long time, as anyone else's life is always more interesting to observe than one's own. I thought of them as *The Couple In The Window*. It could have been the title of a movie. And that is how I watched them, until I pulled the curtains closed and re-entered my own life.

Who would serve my dinner? Sitting on the bed, I reached for *No Dollars Etc.* beside me on the night table and for the hundredth time thumbed through the restaurant section. I searched but nothing appealed to me. Finally, giving up, I blindly threw the book across the room, not caring where it landed. Screw it. I was sick of that damned book. I was sick of trying to live well and pay little. It didn't work. Anywhere. And restaurants in Copenhagen were expensive.

I got dressed, this time comfortably in slacks and a thick wool sweater, my warm leather boots, the things I usually wore at home. I would go out and I would eat a very good, very expensive meal. I pulled the door aggressively shut and ran to the elevator.

I was starved.

Chapter 2

I hadn't meant to stay out so late, or to drink so much wine, or go to that jazz club in the first place, but I had eaten a thick, beefy stew for dinner and I needed to walk.

It was still early, about 8:30, when I started out but already nightfall. I walked briskly, alone in the dark, even though I was told my first day in the city, by the aloof woman who worked in the Tourist Information Office, that a woman was safe here, any time—at night, too.

"This isn't America," she added indignantly, before turning her back on me, as if my question about a woman's safety had amounted to a slur on the Danish national character. I hadn't meant to insult the Danish national character, only to protect myself. It was true, as a single American woman, I was not used to safety. This was a safe place, even for a wandering, solitary woman. Yet I couldn't shed my cultural patterns overnight. Though I ventured out according to the woman's assurances I remained wary and, on hearing approaching footsteps, I would stop and peer over my shoulder, like a cautious cat.

The club had been noisy and dimly lit. Heavy wooden chairs and long tables placed end to end beer hall style in long rows, filled the large room. The jazz was good, the wine was good. Wine was sold by the bottle and many, many bottles of red wine in varying stages of full to empty cluttered the tables. We were crowded together shoulder to shoulder. One had to turn and stretch one's neck to see the stage. The music was hardly audible above the hollow din, but the overall atmosphere was cozy. The wine had opened my face. I had been aware of smiling often at my neighbors, and the smiles had been contagious. Laughter permeated the air as thickly as the smoggy cigarette smoke, which hung like a forgotten cloud over our heads.

In bed the next morning, I opened my eyes but they refused to focus. I tried to lift my head but it lay on the pillow like a stone. I attempted to raise my arm but my inert body had forgotten how to move. The day of the week completely escaped my mind, and if you asked me my name I would have had to think about it before answering.

I lay like this for as long as I could, and it was only the forces of nature that roused me.

Fortunately no one was in the hallway when I appeared in my bathrobe and slippers, flung my towel cavalierly over one shoulder and hugged it close to my chest with my plastic soap container. Convinced that I looked as disheveled as I felt, I ducked into the bathroom and locked the door. Whom was I hiding from? Surely, I admonished myself, finding relief on the cold toilet, I was being overly self-protective and overly vain.

When I emerged, showered and shampooed, my long wet hair sticking to my head like seaweed, I anticipated the same quick route back to my room. As I approached my door, which was diagonally across from the reception desk, I was stopped by the specter of two strange faces turned towards me, smiling. The man, large, bulky and blond sat behind the desk, which barely contained him. The woman, smaller, pale, wafer thin and also blond, stood in front of the desk, her arms folded over her small chest.

"Hello," they said in unison, still smiling at me.

Though startled, I managed to give them a polite "hello" before I escaped to my room and closed the door firmly behind me. Not until I bent my head to towel dry my hair did it fully register that he was not Mr. Blumendahl behind the desk or she Mrs. Blumendahl in front of it. Who were those people anyway? It was Saturday. Perhaps the Blumendahls took the day off and this couple were their substitutes?

I dressed and on my way out stopped at the desk to settle my bill for the next week. The blond man was still seated at the desk, reading the registry.

"Gut morning," he said, beaming.

And now I inspected his large, puffy face, his fat pink lips, his large blue eyes with the heavy eyelids and baggy circles underneath. He was an enormous man, not fat but massive, as if he had been athletic in his younger days and now, in his early forties, his once active muscles were padded with layers of passive flesh. Surely more than six feet tall, his torso jutted far above the top of the desk.

I returned his "good morning," explaining that I wanted to pay for another week. To which he replied "ja, ja" and told me the cost in krone. As I signed my travelers checks, he quizzed me on my stay so far. What had I done, what had I seen, did I like Copenhagen, responding to my answers with sprinklings of ja's and gut's.

His voice and manner of speaking were quieter and meeker than one would expect from such a large, bull-like man. It stuck out to me like a strange mole because like the mole it didn't belong there. There was something odd about him, and the bull's body with the mouse's voice made me wonder exactly what it was. And where were the Blumendahls?

As I handed him my traveler's checks, I off-handedly asked about them.

"They are gone," he said, preoccupied with counting my money. He put the checks in a cash box and put the cash box in a drawer before looking up at me again. "Vee are the new owners. Vee buy the hotel."

"Gone?" I said, echoing his word.

What did "gone" mean? Gone like dead? I saw the mourners, the empty house, someone taking the antique man and woman salt and pepper shakers off the shelf and packing them in a box to be sent to the thrift shop.

"Ja. Gone."

The phone rang. He excused himself to answer it. "Hotel Blumendahl" was all I understood. His speech was garbled in Danish. His English accent had been thick and barely decipherable.

The Blumendahl's departure stunned me. I stood fixed to the spot. I took it personally, and I felt abandoned. How could they leave me? Should I stay? Would I feel as comfortable with this strange new couple? Where did the Blumendahl's go? There was something wrong and ominous about their leaving though I had no rational reason to feel this way.

"Do you need something?"

The woman materialized from behind me, as if she had landed from the sky. I hadn't heard her footsteps. I turned my attention to her inquisitive face. Her eyes were intensely blue, bluer than I remembered from the morning.

I explained that her husband was just telling me that they had bought the hotel.

"Manfred," she said, gazing at him affectionately although he was still on the phone and didn't notice. "And I am Elke."

"How do you do?" I said. Some instinct in me resisted telling her my name though of course they already knew my name. It was written in the registry. She had offered me her hand, which I shook briefly. It was cool and dry with long bony fingers and weighed next to nothing, yet it dwarfed my puny palm.

Her slight body appeared concave, an effect heightened by her round shouldered posture. Yet there was a strength about her too, very much like the strength of a willow bending and swaying in a strong wind but never breaking.

Manfred hung up the phone. Elke continued to chat with me. I wanted to leave but her fluty, seductive voice held me there, and those piercing, ice blue eyes. I couldn't help staring at her pretty oval face, her shocking Scandinavian blond hair.

"I am Danish," she said, "Manfred is German. And you...?"

"American."

"American, yes. That's what I told Manfred when we saw you this morning. I would love to go to America sometime. And Manfred also. Wouldn't you love to go to America, Manfred?"

"Ja." He nodded and grinned, revealing his canine-shaped teeth.

Fortunately the phone demanded his attention again. Now it was time to leave. The conversation had taken an awkward turn. I was suddenly part of a U.N. delegation. And there was The War again: the Refugees had escaped, the Germans had taken their place, occupying Denmark. The Danes still spoke of it bitterly. Hence the need to explain her German husband?

I told her it was nice meeting her and politely excused myself.

Elke accompanied me to the glass door and held it open for me, usurping Mr. Blumendahl's role

"Do you have everything you need?" she asked, standing on the threshold.

"Yes," I said, pushing the first floor elevator button. "Everything."

She smiled and waved, and, as the automatic door slowly slid closed, I waved back.

Chapter 3

In spite of the biting cold day, I had spent the morning walking the city streets, window shopping for affordable souvenirs for friends and visiting a small art museum, which was one of the items on my list of "things to see" that I could now draw a solid line through. I had put the hotel situation out of my mind and enjoyed the pleasant morning. By noon I was famished and craving Swedish meatballs and noodles or a chunky stew. My feet were now frozen yet carried me to a cafeteria-style restaurant I had been to once before, where I knew the portions were large and the prices were small.

A big place, it was mobbed with dozens of other hungry Saturday shoppers. I waited patiently in the long, slow line at the steam tables, inching my tray to the right every few minutes, indecisively gazing at the food. Smells of cooked purple cabbage, boiled potatoes, meatballs in sweet sauces, and simmering vegetables all fought for my attention. I decided on the meatballs (the deep red chunks in heavy sauce were irresistible), purple cabbage, and tea.

Then the question of where to sit.

My devouring eyes focused on the food, I hadn't noticed that the room was nearly full. One had to hunt for a seat, two together was impossible. Again the seating arrangement was family style at picnic-sized tables. The Danes were absolutely uninhibited about sitting right next to you or across from you, giving you a polite acknowledgment and then going on about their business. I, however, the shy American, felt terribly uncomfortable about squeezing myself in between two strangers at a nearby table. I didn't look at them. I felt exposed but mostly starved, interested only in my food.

People at the table were talking to each other. This made me feel even sillier, sitting there by myself. Before long *No Dollars* jumped out of my bag and onto my tray next to the tea, not a book for acting incognito but it was the only reading matter I had with me. I skipped around, reading about points of interest in cities that I might visit later on–Amsterdam, Paris, London. I read and ate slowly, comfortably invisible again.

I was vaguely aware of people getting up and other people sitting down in their places. I paid little attention. I couldn't have told you if they were men or women. I didn't care. I cared about meatballs and cabbage and the British Museum. I took a sip of tea, I turned the page, skimming it. I skewered a fat meatball, cut it in half with my fork and stuck it in my mouth, then turned back to the book. I had established a distinct repeating rhythm:

fork-food-mouth-book. The droning background voices, the mechanical eating had a hypnotizing effect. I forgot where I was, hardly tasted the food. I unconsciously repeated the pattern–fork-food-mouth-book.

"Tourist?"

The word stabbed me awake, having been flung at me from across the table like a well-aimed dart. I picked up my head. A diminutive elderly woman was sipping soup from a large spoon and staring at me.

I stared back.

"Tourist?" The second time she was louder and more insistent.

"Yes," I muttered, slamming shut the guidebook and quickly burying it in my shopping bag underneath the table.

I concentrated on the half-finished lunch and ate it seriously, staring down at my plate, hoping this would end her interrogation.

"You're from the U.S., aren't you?" she asked, as I chewed a piece of meatball.

I "mmmed."

Her English was fluent, with a strong Danish accent but that voice, in highly-pitched and scratchy tones, captured my lurid curiosity. I glanced up at her and noticed how scrawny she was, a small face with a long nose, narrow chin, eyes that were a fading, clear blue. Wispy gray hair escaped from under a navy blue felt hat that looked like it had once been a tall hat that someone had stepped on and flattened in several uneven layers. Her tired navy over-coat was infested with wool balls. All this and her spartan lunch made me feel sorry for the poor old creature and I let down my guard. She seemed harmless enough, if a little eccentric. That hat.

"I've been to America," she said, "to Kansas. My brother moved there thirty years ago. He married an American. Have you ever been to Kansas?"

I said that was interesting and no, I had never been to Kansas. She was quiet again and buttered a piece of flat, dark bread. She took a big bite which puffed out her pallid cheeks. She chewed and watched me as I continued to pick at my plate. I intrigued her, but why? A tourist eating lunch in a cafeteria.

"Have you seen The Little Mermaid?"

The screechy, gravelly voice was difficult to ignore.

I told her I hadn't. Indeed, I hadn't. The Little Mermaid was deliberately not on my list, precisely because it was *the* biggest tourist attraction in Copenhagen. And big deal, a statue in a harbor.

She lowered her spoon and raised her eyebrows.

"You haven't seen The Little Mermaid?!"

I again assured her negatively. How could I have explained myself to her? She would not have understood that I was not really a tourist but an adventuress, not seeing the sights but having life experiences, which did *not* include seeing The Little Mermaid.

"You must see The Little Mermaid," she insisted.

Now my eyebrows rose.

She checked her watch and leaned closer to me.

"I have time. You come with me. I will take you to see The Little Mermaid."

For the first time in that city I experienced fear. It grabbed me in the gut, and my lunch began to feel heavy. The Tourist Office had advised me not to fear the men. They had said nothing about the women of Copenhagen. First the one at the red light and now this one. I began to suspect a malevolent conspiracy led by an army of bossy women who were determined to ruin my trip and rob me of my freedom. The last thing I wanted to do at that moment was to go anywhere with this bird and least of all to the Langelinie harbor to see The Little Mermaid.

I warmly declined her thoughtful invitation, adding that I couldn't possibly trouble her.

"No trouble. I have time."

At that she pushed back her chair, grabbed her tray and stood up, gesturing for me to follow.

"But..." I began but couldn't think of a believable excuse fast enough, as she continued to wildly direct me to leave, pointing with her tray of dirty dishes.

The people still eating at the table looked up at us. I imagined the scene my further resistance would have produced: me protesting, she urging me on, louder and louder.

I stood up.

We deposited our trays at the busing table. Then I

followed her outside, where I hoped to part ways, but the next instant she clutched the sleeve of my coat with her claw-thin fingers, shouting, "Hurry, I see the bus," and pulled me across the street.

I couldn't escape the woman's spell. Every move I made to retreat swept me farther along. I wanted to avoid making a scene, and it was easier to appease her than to fight her. Feeling trapped, I threw up my hands to the fates and boarded the bus.

I chose a window seat. The old woman sat down beside me, pleased with herself. Sitting very straight, she held her black leather purse on her lap with both hands, like a fragile package. She had folded the short strap neatly over the tarnished metal clasp, which locked into a subtle "V".

I readied myself for this trip as I would have for an obligatory visit with distant, boring relations: knowing that it would be a painful experience, I hoped to make it as brief as possible and to find the right excuse to leave when my patience ran out.

The bus jerked into gear, and the old woman leaned toward me.

"This is a good bus. It will take you right to the Langelinie," she shouted, trying to be heard above the churning motor.

"Good," I said, for want of anything better.

"It's not very far."

"Good," I said again, meaning it this time.

"Soon we will come to the Royal Theater. We have the ballet, the symphony, the theater, the opera..."

She rambled on and on, telling me to look at this or that landmark passing by the window. She talked incessantly, acting in her self-appointed role of tour guide. I knew that I would find no excuse to leave and that it would be a very tedious, very long ride. What could I say or do except look in the aforementioned direction, nod my head and "uh, huh" at the appropriate intervals. Not only did she submit me to this sight-seeing tongue-lashing but, to my great embarrassment, she did it in a voice that everyone else on the bus could hear. The adventuress was disarmed and disrobed, reduced to that loathsome status of tourist, being guided no less, as if I were blind, as if I couldn't see for myself what was right in front of my face.

"Look. The King's palace. See? The guards."

Sure enough, we passed what could only be described as a palace, a larger than life, low building made of white stone in the center of which was an enormous circular courtyard, also made of a white but rougher stone, where a number of guardsmen stood at their posts. They were picture book king's guards, in bright red uniforms, long rifles hung on their shoulders, and those curious enormous black fur hats reminiscent of a beaver sitting on one's head that royal guards always seem to wear for no apparent reason other than to look absurd.

The bus stopped at a red light and I watched. I was intrigued by the palace. I'd forgotten about the king, who was actually a political figure in today's world and not a fairy tale character. Two men in long overcoats carrying brief-cases walked across the courtyard. Nothing could have been more foreign to my American sensibility than kings, palaces, and men with briefcases who worked there.

The light changed to green and the palace quickly became history. My guide was mercifully quiet for the moment. The clean, modern bus hummed along the street, every so often picking up and discharging passengers, who boarded in front and left in the rear in an efficient and orderly manner. I relaxed, sinking into my seat.

I wondered why I was acquiescing to be led to see something that I clearly did not want to see. Perhaps it would turn out to be a pleasant episode. I already could hear myself telling my friends back home how this amusing matron picked me up in a cafeteria and took me on a bus across town to see the famous statue of The Little Mermaid. I would make a joke of it, tell it as a funny story, pointing out the woman's more eccentric features, and we'd all laugh. I would describe it as if it had been one great lark, another great adventure on my exciting European vacation.

In my daydreaming I had closed my eyes. But after only a few minutes peace, I was rudely awakened by a sharp poke on my left shoulder.

"Have you been to the ballet?"

"No."

"You haven't?!" She grasped her pocketbook even

28

tighter, making her fingers turn even more pasty white. "You must see the ballet. The Danish Ballet is the best in the world. And it's cheap—the government contributes."

I assured her that I would put it on my list. This was true. Seeing the Royal Danish Ballet might be a worthy experience, one that I hadn't thought of myself—and it was cheap...

"There it is!" She pointed a finger towards the window, her arm so close to my chest that I had to press into my seat to avoid contact.

Instead of retrieving her arm, she reached up and pulled the stop cord. The bell rang and the bus stopped right in front of the theater. She demanded that I go with her.

Now that I had resigned myself to this trip and felt comfortable in the seat, I was reluctant to get off, and I hesitated. However, she once again ordered me to "hurry" and once more I obediently trailed after her, off the bus, across the wide sidewalk and up the many stone steps of the Royal Theater. All the while she was explaining that this was for my benefit, to assure me a ticket for next week's performance, to get a good seat, to see the performance of my choice.

I hardly had a chance to admire the interior of the theater, which was indeed very old and very grand, before she whisked me across the immense and magnificent lobby, like a mother duck with her duckling following close behind, and straight to the box office, where a young woman sat behind a steel barred window and talked on the telephone. Glancing up at me, she pointed to the upper wall and told me to pick a seat.

I looked up and saw high up on the huge wall, a large seating chart of the theater. It was an enormous hall, with the usual orchestra section, two sets of balconies, and tiers and tiers in the gallery. Below the chart was the price list, in krone, which I quickly exchanged in my head into dollars. True, the prices were cheaper than one would expect to pay for comparable seating in the States, but I was disappointed to note that orchestra and balcony seats were still beyond my vacation budget and I resigned myself to any seat in the gallery, which really was cheap, especially in dollars.

To the right and left of the window were the performance schedules and I arbitrarily chose the next Friday evening's program, all of them being equally unfamiliar and, therefore, equally appealing to me.

The little crow woman stood behind me as I stepped up to the window. The ticket-seller seemed bored with my selection, asked me in a bland and chilly voice if so and so row was acceptable and stared at my face waiting for my answer. Without checking the chart, I said that the seat was fine if only to get away from her cool, dispassionate eyes.

I paid for the ticket and secured it in the billfold section of my wallet. My companion was clucking as I followed her outside again.

We were descending the steps when she checked her watch and loudly gasped, as if she were giving out her last breath.

"The time. Ah. I will be late." She hobbled quickly down the remainder of the wide steps.

Late for what? Where could she possibly be going? And why had her time suddenly run out?

When I reached the sidewalk, she instructed me to wait there for the next bus, she had to go now. That was that. No apology, no good-bye, no "nice meeting you." She simply turned around and sped up the street on her petite bird legs.

I stood at the bus stop, watching the raven blue coat, the squashed hat shrink into the distance.

I should have been relieved to be rid of her. I could have gone wherever I wanted, but I remained, feeling much as I did after the inexplicable disappearance of the Blumendahls: abandoned. It didn't seem right going on without her. Going at all had been her idea. And, yet, now the harbor felt like an inevitable destination—my Fate.

The bus appeared, and the door opened in front of me.

I entered and paid the fare. I took a window seat and craned my neck around as far as possible to see where the old woman went, but by then she had flown off on her dark blue wings, vanished as abruptly as she had first appeared at my table.

There were fewer people on this bus. The streets were

also less populated and less residential. The rest of the ride remained deadly silent without that recent cawing in my ear. Now I missed this chatter on the increasingly vacant bus. By the time we got to the harbor only myself and a dock worker remained. The dock worker had gotten on the bus not long before the end of the ride and sat across from the bus driver. They spoke to each other every once in a while like old chums. He bounded off the bus and went directly to a large warehouse at the end of a long pier.

The bus driver watched me step down then slammed the door shut behind my back (before I could change my mind?), put his foot on the gas, turned the bus around and drove away before I had reached the promenade.

I approached the sea. It was an alien sea, cold and uninviting, its damp winds stinging me, making me colder. A long, flat walkway bordered by a thick metal railing and a row of trees stretched the length of the harbor. One could walk for quite a while. It would have been a pleasant walk in warmer seasons.

I gazed at the ocean and imagined these seasons. I imagined myself walking by a warmer ocean, smelling newly-bloomed flowers, listening to trees sighing with the breezes overhead, watching the sun dipping into the horizon, the spectacular sky glowing in sensual colors, breathing the salty sea air. It would be an intoxicating walk. I could see it, feel it, taste it. The harbor was a beautiful, serene place, and I cursed the fate that had sent me there in foul weather.

It felt even colder when I arrived at the water's edge. The wet icy wind burned my face. I wrapped my scarf tightly around my neck, hiked my collar up to my ears and reached in my pockets for the fur-lined leather gloves, which I had removed on the over-heated bus. I stood at the railing, holding onto it with both hands, as if I would be swept up into the air currents if I didn't, and looked out at the cold, gray sea and the cold, gray sky. No ships passed to fill in the otherwise empty scene. No birds flew to liven the deadpan horizon. The sea rolled endlessly towards me and the sky hung still like a flat, heavy curtain.

As I stood at the railing I wished it were summer, the height of summer. I suddenly longed for hot sand and cool water, a bright, steamy day, to be wearing only a bathing suit, my hot skin exposed, feeling light and free. I wanted to be hot, then to be cool. I wanted both—the longing for the water and the relief of it. I wanted to dive into a rolling wave like a big fish, come up for air and go under again. I would be a leaping, happy porpoise, I would rejoice in my solitary swim, I would be satisfied.

This was not to be, at the tail end of winter, wrapped in many layers of protective clothing against the bitter cold, thousands of miles from home. Again I blamed the cruel fate that had sent me to the right place at the wrong time.

Bored with watching the emptiness, I looked around me to see if maybe in the interim someone else had arrived.

I saw no one. Then, turning back to the ocean, I noticed a speck in the corner of my left eye–someone I hadn't seen at first?–and with renewed interest turned again to see, to my great surprise, that it was not a person at all: it was the statue–The Little Mermaid–at quite a distance, on the edge of the shoreline. I'd almost forgotten about her. How had I missed her? I had given the harbor a quick initial survey and, not seeing her, I figured she was out of sight, further down or around a bend somewhere. To discover she had been there all along was shocking, and terrifying. I felt that the statue had snuck up on me the way intrusive women were continuing to sneak up on me in this city. Was this my destiny here, to be surrounded by a league of strange women everywhere I turned? Not big scary Amazons, but women my own size, endless reflections of myself, as if I were standing inside a room of mirrors. This reflection wasn't even alive.

I eyed her from a distance, still so amazed at how I could have missed her that the thought of getting a closer look wasn't my first impulse. I wanted to understand my oversight. Of course, once the blinders of surprise were lifted, it was quite obvious: she was so small, so human-sized. I had been expecting to see an imposing womanly figure that dominated the seascape. Instead, I had found a small girl.

As I approached her, I unrealistically kept expecting her to grow larger than life-sized the closer I got, but she remained proportionately small.

She was an adolescent girl. Even on her rock, she only reached my chest and I had to look down at her. She was a real mermaid, half-naked, a fishtail instead of legs, and totally unprotected from the ocean, the weather, or passing admirers, which again surprised me. I had envisioned her either caged by an enclosure or ringed by grass and a railing, at the least skirted by a bed of flowers, somehow guarded and unapproachable. There she was, small and delicate, exposed and vulnerable, and, like the mermaid in the fairy tale, forlornly looking out to sea for her unattainable lover, longing for legs, longing to be human.

The sculpture was very realistic and it sat naturally on a real boulder. Her hair looked wet and clung close to her head and neck, as if she had just leapt out of the sea, and her skin looked warm and soft in spite of its metallic green patina. I felt an urge to touch her, to make sure, as if my mind could not believe the simple truth of what my eyes could see: a metal girl on a rock.

I looked around me quickly. I saw no one, and the only sounds I heard were the watery rushing crescendos of the sea. I knelt down to meet her at eye level. I took off my glove and reached out to her with my forefinger, touching her cheek with my fingertip.

The ice cold of the metal shot through me like an electric jolt.

It took me a second to pull my finger away, as if I had touched something hot instead of cold. My hand was freezing and I thrust my stiff fingers back into my glove.

How stupid of me! What an absurd thing to do! Of course she was cold. Was I crazy? I stood up, shivering in the icy sea wind. I was still berating myself, when I noticed an ancient gentleman in an enormous overcoat with a thick, wide scarf wrapped many times around his neck, who was standing farther down, by the railing and leaning on a heavy wooden cane in the shape of the number seven. He was watching me, as if *I* were The Little Mermaid, as if *I* were the curiosity.

Was he grinning at me, too? I couldn't be sure from that distance. It was one thing to be foolish and another to be discovered being foolish. Had he been watching me the whole time? Where had he come from and how long was he going to stand there, rigid as a statue, scrutinizing me? Just as I thought this the statue man came to life, waved a hand at me, and walked on.

I stood up and turned to go, needing to get out of there as fast as I could. I'd had enough of this place, of mermaids, of goblins suddenly materializing.

I walked fast then ran to the bus stop. I couldn't get there fast enough. I was running and thinking yes, the man had laughed at me, and the statue had, too. Frozen on her rock, she was a mockery of love's longings, of all notions of unattainable ideals. She would sit there, waiting forever, and never, never get what she wanted. I was running and thinking how stupid this was. How very stupid.

I ran all the way to the bus stop and stood there catching my breath, relieved to be going back to the city, to the normal. The bus stop felt safe, home base.

Calmer now I reflected how we both seemed foolish: the Mermaid, aching to be human when she was only a fish, and I, aching to be a fish when I was only human. I dismissed the incident and The Little Mermaid before the bus had even arrived.

But the bus didn't come for a long while.

I waited impatiently at the bus stop. I was bitterly cold, painfully cold. Folding into myself, I turned my head away from the damp wind slapping my face. From the ocean and its callings. From The Little Mermaid. I'd seen her now, and as I'd said all along, it was no big deal.

Chapter 4

At breakfast the next morning, the first thing I noticed was that Elke was wearing the same gray, tight-fitting sweater and the same matching drab gray skirt as the day before. (Did she have a limited wardrobe, or did she just not care?) The second was that she chose to sit across the table from me and eye me above the rim of her coffee cup every time she took a sip between her wide, Scandinavian lips. She stared, as if the liquid in the cup was a vast sea and I the small dark figure of a ship on its horizon, which she was scrutinizing. She should have been squinting, her gaze was so fixed and intent. I felt the most uncomfortable sensation of being spied on, not from across the table, but surreptitiously, from a distance with binoculars.

"You are late this morning," she said, smiling questioningly and returning the cup to its cracked saucer.

"Yes, I overslept. I didn't think I was going to make it to breakfast."

She could spy on me all she liked. The fact was that I had nothing to hide. My explanation was perfectly honest. I did not have a wild and crazy night. I was merely exhausted from walking for hours, which I was not used to doing, and ended up overtired. The cold linoleum floor had not invited me out of bed. The weather and economics had forced me up that morning. I did not want to buy breakfast, which meant wandering about in the winter rain.

Elke served the same customary continental breakfast as the Blumendahls: small hard rolls with butter and jam, a pot of strong coffee accompanied by a miniature pitcher of real cream and an abundant bowl of sugar cubes, all at one end of the long, narrow table where we sat and rested our elbows on the old yellow flowered oilcloth. To avoid the rain, I pondered an indoor activity for the day, which at 9:45 a.m. already was dank and dismal.

I might have asked Elke what she was doing there drinking coffee at that hour. She was usually breezing through the halls, changing sheets and vacuuming and such. However, it was not Elke's comings and goings that interested me; I was more avidly curious about her wearing the same shabby outfit two days in a row, and whatever did she find attractive about Manfred, that giant milk cow of a mate?

Elke helped herself to another cup of coffee. She smiled at me again, as she poured and stirred the cream, rather roughly. The only other breakfaster, one of the boarders, got up and left the room. Her icy blue eyes escorted him out the door, then returned to me.

"Tell me," she said, "are you always traveling alone?"

"Not always," I answered, buttering half a roll.

"You're not lonely?"

"Oh, no. It's fine, really. I like traveling by myself. I can explore. It's much freer."

I truly believed this, in spite of the fact that I had never traveled at all before, let alone by myself. Nonetheless, I thought it quite a suitable answer to Elke's question, as I buttered the other half of my roll and took a large bite.

Elke quietly watched me eat for a few minutes, still eyeing me across her dark sea.

I assumed a carefree attitude, trying to enjoy this meager breakfast in spite of Elke, though I felt about as carefree as a fly caught on flypaper.

"Do you have a 'friend' at home?" Elke asked, which, for her, was a perfectly logical transition. She possessed the remarkable ability to start a conversation in the middle.

"What?"

"At home, do you have a man friend?"

"A boyfriend?"

"Yes." She smiled expectantly.

"No," I answered honestly.

"No? Such a pretty girl like you? And so young..."

I shrugged. Even I didn't fully understand it. Anyway, this was the only response I felt like giving. Elke's question had an accusatory ring to it, and I resented her prying. I didn't owe her an explanation. I could have lied if I had wanted to, fabricated a boyfriend, a story. I was a free woman. Let her think what she liked.

Elke raised her cup and examined me once more. She took a sip of coffee then matter-of-factly returned the cup to the saucer.

"You need a man," she insisted.

"A man?" I stared at her wide-eyed and incredulous. The cheek.

"Yes. You are too much alone."

"I'm fine. I told you—I like being alone."

"I know what you are doing in your room. You need a man."

She knew? What did she know? How did she know? Was she joking?

"Excuse me." I slid my chair back and glanced at my watch. "I have to get going."

"I am only trying to help."

"Thank you, but I'm fine."

As I was about to walk out the door Elke said, "I just want to see you happy here. You will have a good time."

I turned around to face her.

"I'm having a *won*derful time. 'See you."

I bolted to my room. I longed to be outside, rain or not.

I needed a man. The nerve. She knew what I was doing in my room. Really...She couldn't. It's true that their room was next to mine, but I never made a sound... What was she doing? Listening with an ear to the wall?

Chapter 5

The National Museum was the perfect choice–solid, quiet, warm, and very dry. It was so large that seeing it could easily take up most of my day, not that I was much of a museum-goer, hardly at all. But where else does a solitary Woman-of-the-World go on a rainy, chilling winter day in wonderful, wonderful Copenhagen? Whoever wrote that song must have been there in summer, because in winter, Copenhagen was about as wonderful as my cold, wet feet.

I could fool myself that I was interested in the exhibits more easily than I could fool myself that profound independence sometimes didn't produce a profound longing for companionship. Staring at broken pottery and antique furniture, the ruins of former civilizations, was much better than acknowledging my own ruinous state of mind.

Elke had rattled me. I was not used to such intrusiveness. She was both coy and bold, appealing and repelling, and thoroughly, shockingly unpredictable. I could not understand this personality or her interest me—a guest, a transient outlander.

The stuffy atmosphere of the museum was putting me to sleep. After a few hours, my feet were wearing as thin as the soles of my shoes, and I could not read one more description of one more relic or stare past the glare into one more glass display case. I wandered down the cavernous hallway and looked for a room with a chair. At the end of the corridor, I took a left through an identical hallway, from which I heard strange bellowing sounds. These low airy moans, like old trees crying in the wind, drew me forward. It was a haunting siren's sound, if you might imagine what that would be like, not pretty or pleasant to listen to but nonetheless captivating. Long-lasting low drones, then higher ones, floated in the air for minutes at a time.

The eerie music beckoned me to a large room of floor-to-ceiling glass cases full of bowed horns with elongated narrow necks and small mouths. Evidently, it was the sounds of these horns that I heard being piped into the room.

They were Viking horns, and these were the sounds of ancient Scandinavia. How intriguing. Even more intriguing was a cushioned bench in the center of the room.

I sat down in the middle of the bench. The pervasive music continued. The Vikings had come back to play their horns, unwilling to keep their centuries old silence. They blew with a hollow, unearthly beauty, the yearnings of an ardent wind through a canyon, unlike any musical sound I had ever heard.

Soon my feet stopped throbbing, and, listening to the music, I experienced that pleasant, empty mind state when one listens intently, in the moment. It was an effect similar to that of meditating, which I had briefly tried a few years back when it seemed that everyone I knew was practicing some form of meditation, although I could never overcome my restlessness to get anywhere with it. The moment struck me that way—at once immediate and timeless.

A man who looked about my age came into the room. Perhaps the horns had beckoned him, too. He edged his way slowly across the first glass case. He appeared to be genuinely curious about the display of horns, and genuinely uncurious about me. He hadn't turned around.

I could only see his curly dark hair and the back of his thick down parka, a deep royal blue. He was tall with an athletic build, but thin like a swimmer or tennis player. His large black boots laced up the front, and his coat smelled like the rain—cold and pungent.

He made his way to the second case. I stood up and examined the contents of the first case, casually inching my way to the right, where he was standing. The horns were still blowing overhead. I stole a few furtive looks at him.

I edged my way to the right, until I stood at his side. He was a good head taller than I. His cologne, a sweet, earthy scent like musky sandalwood, wafted down over me.

I glanced at him again but this time I caught his eye and he smiled.

"Quite a sound, isn't it?" I asked, assuming that he spoke English like most Danes.

"Yes, I like it," he answered in a distinctive American accent.

"Oh, you're American? Where are you from?"

"Minnesota. And you?"

"New England."

"Nice country." He nodded then turned back to the cases, hands still in his pockets. He had given me a warm smile, which made me notice the deep brown eyes framed in thick lashes, the high cheekbones with ruddy cheeks. He could easily have been a skier. His head was covered only by the dark chestnut fur of his own, wooly and sensually curly locks that spilled over the collar of his jacket.

Have you been here long?" I asked, as if there had been no interruption in our former conversation.

"About a week," he said, still examining the contents of the case.

"You?"

"About the same, a little more. Are you traveling alone?"

He turned and faced me again.

"Yeah, just me. I'm pretty independent."

"Me, too. That is, I'm alone, too. I really love it. It's so freeing. Don't you think?"

"I guess it is, if that's what you want. Well, have a good trip."

He smiled at me again, departed down the corridor

and was quickly out of sight.

Just then the horn sounds stopped. There was an end to them after all.

I couldn't stay in the room, which now felt deathly quiet. I half-heartedly rambled through a few more exhibits and left. Somehow, the empty museum had lost its sense of comfort for me.

Outside, the rain had stopped but the sky was covered with dense clouds. The air felt misty and cold, a nasty, threatening kind of cold. I looked for a café and spent the rest of the afternoon drinking tea by the pot full and reading a paperback. It was a little downstairs place that sold bread and pastries. There, at a table covered in a red-checkered tablecloth next to the window, as busy feet passed by, I sat reading, sipping tea, and watching the gray day grow blacker with every passing hour.

I managed to stay out well into the evening, browsing in shops, having a leisurely dinner and wandering around the city.

Copenhagen at night seemed more cheery, colorful and well lit, especially so in the dead of winter after those cheerless days. I was getting used to being on the streets alone at all hours, finally feeling safe. It was true: no one ever bothered me. Other people, women, went about their business, not concerned about anyone else on the street. I didn't sense the usual tension and paranoia of a U.S. city at night. I had let down my guard and lost track of the time.

I also had lost my sense of direction for a while and mysteriously found myself in a residential neighborhood, where a small carnival was set up on a large plot of ground. It was one of those temporary affairs, the kind that moves around like a circus train, not too different from the ones I was used to in the States—Ferris wheel and other rides, quaint carnival music, chance booths with prizes of stuffed animals.

I paid the small fee and entered the gate. I couldn't resist a homey neighborhood carnival on a clear winter night. The boisterous noises and rainbow-colored lights were a welcome change from the quiet. I wanted to join the people around me who were having a good time. I needed some fun.

I passed the booths, the hawkers, the excited, laughing children and their parents. No one seemed to mind the cold. This suddenly struck me as eccentric, a carnival in winter, then made good sense. What better way to enliven a dull season?

Off the aisle by the booths was a low shelter that looked like a chicken coop. I stepped inside. People were busily cranking the arms of slot machines. Teenagers as well as adults fed the slots with coins, looking expectantly at the gaping mouths. Stuffed animals and other prizes hung from the ceiling. I thought it odd that there were slot machines at a fair and that children could play with them. The carnival attendant, wearing an apron with pockets full of change, approached me, assuming that I had come in to play.

He said something to me in Danish, then seeing that I didn't understand him, he translated, "Do you need the coins?"

"No, thank you. I'm just watching."

"It doesn't cost more to play. Why don't you play?"

"No, thank you, really; I can't afford to lose any money," I said with a polite chuckle.

"Money? Ah, you think we gamble. No, no, it's against the law. Look, we play with these. It costs nothing."

He held out to me a handful of coins from his apron pocket. They were slugs.

"You play with these, you win this," he said, pointing to the prizes.

I studied his face, then I glanced around at the people standing in front of the slot machines and turned back to him. Still smiling, he handed me the slugs.

I felt foolish, but then, how would I know that gambling was illegal, in a city, in a country that abounded in sex shops?

I took the slugs.

Finding an unoccupied machine that was as far away as I could get from anyone else, I dropped a slug into the slot. I felt a little silly, not really knowing why I was doing this. But as I poured the make-believe coins into the coin slot, as I pulled the arm down, as the fruits spun around in the eye sockets of the machine, I began to enjoy myself.

I wasn't thinking about a prize or money. I was happy to lose myself for an hour in a truly purposeless pursuit, and I felt thoroughly amused.

I stood for the longest time, feeding slugs to the machine and cranking the arm. I felt ridiculous but content. I had nothing to lose, not money, not time, not pride. What better way to end an otherwise useless day? I inwardly laughed at the prophetic justice of my situation. I laughed and played with the hungry slot machine that ate all my slugs.

When I returned to the hotel the two boarders were huddled around the TV, the one, a paunchy man with a puffy, basset hound face, and the other a tall, lean man with dirty blond hair that flopped over on one side of his head as if he were wearing a poorly fitting toupee. Both were drinking beer from portly green bottles. The heavier man was sitting quietly cradled into the rounded arm of the loveseat, while the tall one stood between the TV and him, holding the beer bottle in one outstretched arm and gesturing with his free hand at the set, talking in an abnormally loud voice, either angry or impassioned about something, on the show, I assumed.

Elke and Manfred sat by themselves at the end of one of the breakfast tables on the other side of the room. They were also drinking beer from taller, mahogany colored bottles, although Elke sipped hers from a glass. I passed by the door and poked my head in. They both smiled and waved to me and invited me to join them.

I politely declined and continued to my room. I did

not want to sit with them, though in my gleeful mood, I even began to be amused with them. They weren't so bad, really. Ekle had probably meant well. She was just somewhat peculiar. And, it was true, that every time I saw her, I couldn't help notice how very pretty she was, so classically Scandinavian—those wide sensual lips, those electric eyes.

I should have been exhausted, but I wasn't. Cranking the slot machine had cranked me up. I was more restless than anything. I tossed my bag on the bed, took off my coat and threw it next to the bag. Then I fell into the upholstered chair and let out a deep sigh.

Like a slug lying hidden underneath a rock, there was an undeniable truth underneath that sigh: I was bored. How could I be, after a day so full of activity? At least it felt like activity, going from here to there, doing this and that. Maybe it hadn't added up to much in the end, activities being on the outside of things.

I stood at the sink and washed my face. Then I combed my hair, as if grooming could restore my sense of purpose. I looked at the uneven walls, but they didn't look back at me. They were blind and unconscious. Someone walked by my room and down the hall, slamming shut the bathroom door. Then I heard the sprinklings of the shower. I could also hear the muffled voice of my neighbor conversing with the TV set.

I stood at the window and pulled the curtains aside, hoping to see *The Couple In The Window*. Their light blazed, but the drapes were drawn shut, and all I could see was a pale blue rectangle.

This disappointed me. I suddenly longed for their picture of conjugal complacency. Of course, why this domesticated couple fascinated me was the question. Theirs was the common situation, not a life that I had ever envisioned for myself. In fact, my vision for my life was quite cloudy. I had a stronger sense of what I didn't want than what I did want. Yet, I felt a primal longing for this unknown way of being.

Becoming a Woman-of-the-World was proving to be more difficult and complicated than I had imagined.

I dropped the curtains and faced my room again. It was prim and tidy. The twin beds had been made with their covers taut and unwrinkled. The harsh overhead lamp revealed the shabby furniture in a most unflattering light.

What now? I asked myself. What does a Woman-of-the-World do when she comes home and finds herself in this condition? I pondered this for a moment. Certainly, I concluded, she goes out again—into the World.

Dressed once more in my coat and shoulder bag, I inspected myself in the mirror but quickly turned away. The light truly was unflattering.

Chapter 6

I went back to that club, Montmartre. I had liked it. I had always liked jazz clubs. This one was friendly and had made me feel at ease.

An American group had packed the house that evening. Jazz is popular in Europe, and American jazz is the most popular. They were a black group from New York.

The band was playing some standards when I sat down. I could have been in America, I could have been anywhere.

I recognized the same gray cloud of smoke hanging above the tables, evidently a regular of the club. The noises were the same; the same bottles of wine cluttered the same dark tables. Good. Finally something was familiar.

I ordered a glass of red wine. I couldn't have managed a whole bottle by myself or even a carafe. I wasn't much of a wine drinker. Two goblets would probably see me through the evening.

I leaned my elbows on the table and faced right to see the band, a typical quartet—saxophone, bass, drum, the singer playing piano. They were pretty good, from what I could hear above the noisy crowd.

When the waiter came, the band was playing what sounded like an Ellington tune, something warm and dreamy. I sipped the wine and rocked my head gently to the rhythm of the song. I leaned back in my chair. I must have been grinning because the woman sitting across from me smiled at me as though I had just smiled at her. So this time I did, then turned my attention back to the music. I listened for a while. The band was still playing the same song, a very long version with a few solo interludes. I listened and drank wine.

The woman across the table had been engaged in a lively conversation with the man who sat to my right. I hadn't noticed him until I saw them talking, which now struck me as odd, since he was a rather large, solid type. I assumed that he was her date, but if he was I wondered why he sat across the table like that, not even in front of her. He had a short neat beard and sandy-colored hair and reminded me of an illustration of a kindly woodsman in a children's book, with rosy cheeks and full, rosy lips, which probably was the result of wine more than fresh air. Two wine bottles made a fence between him and the woman, one empty, one nearly empty, with maybe a glass left.

They appeared to be arguing about something, but it was a friendly argument because every once in a while they would laugh, either at what they had just said themselves or at what the other had just said. I liked them. They were as entertaining as the band. I found myself enjoying their parrying banter in spite of the fact that I couldn't understand a word of it.

They saw me watching them and stopped talking. The woman turned to me, smiling again.

"Do—you—know—this—band?" she said in a magnetic accent, haltingly, punctuating every word, as if each word were a complete sentence. She was a little drunk, but pleasantly so. She was beginning to lose her sense of balance.

"No, I don't. But I don't know much about jazz bands."

Of course she had spoken to me in English, seeing me as a foreigner, even half-crocked. What was it about me that made me seem foreign? Was it my long hair? By now I had noticed that most Danish women had short, fashionable hairdos, like this woman. She had atypical brunette and very thick hair cut neck length. This with her small, chiseled face made her look vaguely like a beautiful courtly page. Thick, dark eyebrows outlined large deep blue eyes, a true midnight blue.

"You-are-American?"

"Yes."

"I am telling my friend here," she said, pointing to the man next to me and still talking in her staccato style, "they are the *best* band to come here. They are *so* good. He likes another band, a Danish band. I tell him these Danes will never play jazz like the Americans. We are always disagreeing but we are still laughing. What do you think?

They are good? Please excuse my very bad English."

"I think they're very good—and your English is fine."

"You see, Olaf? You see? You know *nothing*. This girl knows; she is American. She knows jazz."

"It's not true, I really don't know anything about jazz," I began to explain to poor Olaf.

However, poor Olaf wasn't offended in the least. He was laughing.

"Don't worry, she is only teasing me. We're good friends. She is so drunk she won't remember what she is saying tomorrow."

"I-am-not-drunk, Olaf," the woman said, with a little pout.

"No, you are not drunk, and you will not remember what you said tomorrow."

"Oh, you," she said, pouring herself the last glass of wine.

"Come, you have had enough."

He tried to take the bottle away from her, but she was too quick for him. She poured the last drop of wine into her glass, and he frowned at her in a concerned way.

"I am not drunk," she insisted and drank more wine.

"She isn't always like this," he said. "She is a nice woman. She has been my best friend, for many years. She is having a hard time."

She liked this and smiled at him, taking a liberal gulp of wine.

"Olaf is *my* best friend. And I am having a hard time.

He is the best one, though. He is such a friend. Everyone should have such a friend. He is taking very good care of me. He is a good, good man. He is a *prince*."

I turned to see Olaf's reaction to this.

He smiled at her in his affectionate woodsman's way and raised his wine glass to his lips.

"My name is Elizabeth," she said to me, extending her hand across the table, "and this is Olaf, of course."

Olaf offered me his hand, which was large and warm. His grasp was gentle and comforting.

I introduced myself then couldn't help remarking how surprised I was that a Danish woman would be named "Elizabeth."

She rolled her eyes and said, "My mother loves the queen." Then she laughed and added "and I am Swedish".

Which must have been quite a joke between them because Olaf laughed with her for a while.

I, of course, missed the point of this but joined in with them as best as I could.

The band took a break and left the stage. The din of conversation filled the room again as waiters, like persistent hound dogs, sniffed out more orders of wine.

"You-will-drink-wine-with-us?" Elizabeth asked me and flagged a waiter before I could accept, Olaf protesting again that she had had enough, and Elizabeth pooh-poohing him with a wave of her hand.

Olaf turned to me, with one wary eye on Elizabeth

and said in a low voice, "She will be very sorry tomorrow. She is very unhappy."

I was confused by these little asides of his about Elizabeth, by this candidness, which, I was learning, was a Danish characteristic, as if the private life was nothing sacred, was something to be shared at large, even with a stranger. Though, I had to admit, I wanted to know more about Elizabeth.

When the wine arrived we drank a toast to American jazz. This wine was different than what I had been drinking, a decent red wine, tangy and dry. I drank it liberally, since there was now a large full bottle, and I wanted to be more like them. The wine made me less self-conscious and definitely more unglued. I also decided to try another new taste—a taste of Danish candor, to me an even more seductive and intoxicating potion than the alcohol.

Staring into the midnight of Elizabeth's eyes I asked, "Why are you having a hard time?"

Elizabeth gave me a wry smile and raised her glass to her lips for a shot of wine before she answered me.

"I lost my job, now I had to move, to a not so good flat, small, in Christianshavn. Not so good place. You say, working class. The fishermen live there."

She said this in a tone that was more self-deprecating than condescending to the fisherman, and with the same little wry smile, as if her situation also amused her somehow, if only ironically.

She started to raise her glass again but Olaf interrupted

by saying, "Elizabeth stop it. Enough. You will be sick," and this time she listened to him and put the glass back on the table. Such was the case already: her eyes were turning an opaque ceramic blue.

"I'm sorry to hear that," I said, in a feeble attempt to save her from further embarrassment, although I still seemed to be the only one susceptible to that emotion. "I hope you find something soon. What kind of work do you do?"

"I...."

"She is a poet. A *poet*," Olaf said, butting in.

"The Poet of the Fishermen," Elizabeth said, raising her glass to announce her title and carefully replacing it on the table without drinking again.

I must have looked bewildered because she then added, "Olaf is helping to get a job for me, in his office. He is a, a...Olaf what do you call in English your work?"

"Graphic designer," he said. "We have a studio. She can do something. She needs the work."

I was really beginning to like this Olaf. He was a prince, as Elizabeth had said, and I couldn't help wondering why they weren't more than friends, perhaps married.

"Are-you-married?" Elizabeth asked me suddenly, as if she were reading my thoughts.

Elizabeth spoke in a ponderously slow, punctuated manner. Her English was faltering, and her disintegrating state of mind added to the difficulty. Even so, her voice had a hypnotizing effect on me. I would soon be lulled into a conscious sleep.

"Oh, no," I answered her. "I'm single. Are you...?"

"Deevorced. He-left-me. For another girl. Else. Very blond, very stupid. She laughs. Ha.Ha! And he is an artist. An artist! He is famous in Denmark. I am not famous. I only am a poet. But they teach me in the university."

"Oh, I'm sorry," was all I could manage to say, though this barrage of information was overwhelming. She certainly was having a hard time, and I couldn't help but identify with her circumstances–poor, left, lost.

I explained to her that I had begun to write some poetry, that I had also recently been dumped by my lover for someone else, that I too was unemployed, lacking in funds and only on this vacation because I simply didn't know what to do next. And, as if this weren't enough, that my middle name was Elizabeth.

"Ah," she said, then spoke excitedly to Olaf in Danish to which he said something back and nodded.

She reached across the table as far as she could and pointed a finger at me.

"You-and-I-are-the-same-girl."

I was charmed by this remark but couldn't think of anything to respond except to point out that "girl" was not the right word to use to refer to me or to her, who was surely in her early thirties, but, of course, I restrained myself and simply said "hmmm."

"We-must-talk-more-when-I-am...am...when-I-can-talk-better. I-am-tired-now. Tomorrow. Meet me tomorrow. At Rådhuspladsen under the clock at twelve o'clock.

You know Rådhuspladsen?"

I assured her I did, the central square, and she was referring to the Town Hall clock. I had passed it almost every day on one route or another.

Olaf eyed her dubiously and muttered in my ear.

"She won't remember. I'll give you the address, her house. You take the 17 bus to Christianshavn. Here."

He fished a small scrap of paper from his pocket on which he started to write down her name, and the street, the letter B, a...

"No," Elizabeth protested. "I won't forget. Stop, Olaf. Don't. I don't want this."

She was so displeased and upset that Olaf actually stopped writing the address and looked at me apologetically. I took the scrap of paper from his hand and discreetly stuffed it into my coat pocket.

"She won't remember. I know her. You'll see." Then turning to her he said, "Come, it's late. You're tired."

He also offered to help me fetch a cab, which I gratefully accepted. The band had stopped playing, and I didn't want to be left behind, only to have to find my solitary way back to the hotel.

We stood on a well-lit but deserted street corner, everyone tired and quiet now, even Elizabeth, who stood up better than I had expected she would.

I was a little tipsy myself from too much wine and the power of Elizabeth's charm, and I was glad for the damp, cold air that brought me down to earth. We assured each other that we had enjoyed meeting and all agreed to meet again. I gave them both the hotel phone number. There were few cabs that time of night and we waited patiently, Elizabeth holding onto Olaf's right arm, I leaning towards his left, and Olaf standing between us straight as the lamppost.

Chapter 7

I had been waiting directly under the Town Hall clock in Rådhuspladsen for what seemed an eon. It was now 12:20 p.m. and no sign of Elizabeth. The day was dark, overcast, and misty. My feet had absorbed the cold from the damp pavement.

The enormous square pulsated with flotillas of people bobbing through it in rushing wavelets. My head was swept left and right, front and back, following every crossing ripple, but no Elizabeth anywhere.

With the mountainous Town Hall building looming behind me, I worried that perhaps it had engulfed me by burying me in its dark brick shadow, and I placed myself more prominently forward. But my prominence proved to be no beacon for the lost ship of Elizabeth.

I paced back and forth, from impatience as well as discomfort, and checked the towering clock again. Five more minutes had passed. I was giving her the long benefit of the doubt, assuming that an anticipated hangover would slow her down this morning and cause her to oversleep.

I continued to pace but stopped short when behind me someone called my name. I turned around to see Olaf at the far corner, vigorously waving his arm at me and running across the square. It took him a minute to reach me, panting and cheerful.

"Good morning," he said, grinning down at me.

"You mean good afternoon," I said, glancing at the clock and eyeing him quizzically.

"She didn't come, yes?"

I nodded, without changing my expression.

"I was home thinking, that good person will be waiting in Rådhuspladsen and Elizabeth will be too sick and forget to come and here I am doing nothing, so why don't I meet her and maybe she will let me take her to lunch?"

I was confused by this sudden change of plans and surprised that the friendly woodsman had become more friendly that I had bargained for. But I didn't mind. It was now past 12:30 and Elizabeth was ominously absent. I was hungry and longed for the warm and dry indoors.

"Are you sure? You don't have to *take* me..."

"No, no I insist. I know a place at Nyhavn, good lunch food. You will like it. Come."

Instead of "coming", I looked wistfully over the square.

"She's not coming," Olaf whispered close to my ear and lead me away by the elbow.

Olaf was right again: I liked the place—a café-style restaurant at Nyhavn, a harbor extension that consisted of a dead end central canal with antique ships and wooden fishing boats and flanked by very old brick townhouses. It had been a dying and disreputable neighborhood that was being respectably resurrected with boutiques and fashionable cafes, like this one. We had a window table with a view of the water and the street. Bright blue linens covered the small tables and the room glowed with light. Modern, brightly colored posters of yachts and ocean scenes in wooden frames sparkled on the clean white walls. The place was so warm and friendly that I forgot my disappointment about not meeting Elizabeth and I thought the sun had begun to shine, but when I looked out the window I saw that the sky was actually still a dull metal gray.

Olaf had ordered for us various smørrebrød, or what they called in English "salat" sandwiches—the typical open-faced affair on dark, thin bread topped with different meats, fish and vegetables drowning in fresh mayonnaise. I had eaten smørrebrød before but this food was particularly delicious, much better than in the cheaper restaurants I had been frequenting. I ate heartily, appreciating Olaf's generosity and good taste.

Olaf applauded the food, asked me if everything was O.K., did I want anything else.

I assured him that I had more than enough to eat and that it was all very good.

He drank coffee and looked happy. He pulled at his beard, which seemed to be a nervous habit, (he had done this a number of times as he read the menu) and continued eating, smiling at me after every few bites.

"I'm happy you came with me. You're such a good person."

"How do you know?"

"Of course you are, to wait so long for Elizabeth, to come with me now. I like you."

I blushed and mumbled "Thank you. I like you, too," for want of anything better to say, although it was basically true. Then I hastily retreated into the food, unused to this kind of naked flattery.

"You're so shy. I'm sorry. Did I say something wrong?"

"No, no really, it's fine..."

Olaf smiled and took a bite of smørrebrød and swallowed it.

"You must get used to us Danes. We say anything on our minds. I think Americans are different. They don't tell what they are thinking. Don't mind me. I'm just one of those Danes."

"I guess I'm just one of those Americans." We laughed.

There was some truth in his observation, and it was the thing that had struck me the most about these people – their frankness and honesty.

"Why is your English so good?" I asked, really curious

now, contrasting it with Elizabeth's tentative fluency and wanting to turn his attention away from me.

"I lived in London for a year, when I was in art school, an exchange program. A long way from my father's farm."

"You grew up on a farm?"

"Yes, in Jutland. But I always wanted to be an artist. My father let me go to university–it's free for everyone here–so I studied art, became a graphic designer. Now I work in a good studio."

I looked at him closely and realized that farmer described him, too. I had to adjust my picture of Olaf, and I couldn't decide whether he was more friendly woodsman or gentleman farmer.

In either case, it was so simple for Olaf–living, that is. One, two, three and there you were. I admired his ease and tranquility with living, perhaps something more foreign to me than his country or culture. I envied him, and I wondered if this tranquility could be absorbed, that if I breathed in Danish air long enough it might overtake me. Or perhaps I could breathe in Olaf.

As I was preoccupied with these musings he was saying, "...And what about you? Your living?"

"My living?" It was a word I never used. A job, yes. But–a living? Even being asked the question indicated to me something lacking. There was uncertainty, clearly – what *was* I doing with my life? There were vague, unclarified longings but no words to express any of this, no answers, only more questions: A living? Was I living?

"I don't know," I answered stupidly enough, further explaining that I had been working in public relations–announcements and brochures–at the University. Then they had to fire people because of budget cuts, so I lost my job.

"Now, I'm not sure. I suppose I could be a journalist. I could go to school."

"But you said last night that you write poetry..."

"It's just something I do." I shrugged, repeating that I didn't know, I didn't know, what did I know about my life anyway?

"It's good not to know," Olaf pronounced. "Then you will be surprised. You'll see."

"You seem to know what you're doing."

"That's because I only know how to do one thing – be a designer. It's really simple-mindedness," a point that he emphasized by tapping his forehead with his finger.

I was charmed by Olaf's humility. I understood why Elizabeth called him a "prince." He was princely–diplomatic, strong, kind, a gentleman. He simply made one feel at ease, and I was grateful for this quality in him.

The café was crowded, and the wooden floor and furnishings amplified the deafening voices that crashed around us. I was content to be quiet and let the sound waves wash over me. When we finished eating, the waiter cleared our dishes and Olaf took the liberty of ordering dessert, as it turned out pastry, more coffee, and shots of Cherry Heering.

I drank the sweet, heavy brandy much too quickly and it burned my throat, then immediately went to my head. Olaf had toasted me to my future.

"And to yours," I echoed, raising my glass again.

He smiled at this but then a more serious look overcame him, darkening his face like one who has suddenly stepped into the shade from bright sunlight. He was quiet as he stared out the window and haphazardly destroyed his pastry with a fork. I wondered if *I* had said something wrong. It was the first time that I had seen him look grave. I didn't pry. I sipped the brandy, alternately watching the street traffic and Olaf's increasingly appealing gentleman farmer/friendly woodsman's face.

When he looked at me again he was still wearing this somber mask. Then he quickly gulped the remains of his drink and asked for two more, to which I tried to object, but once again he won me over, although I was already slowing down and weakening from the first.

When we finished Olaf suggested that we walk around the canal. I agreed that this was a fine idea. However, when I tried to walk I discovered that both my legs and my brain had become rubbery and my head weighed me down. For some reason Olaf noticed this and offered his forearm for me to grab hold of since his hands were in the pockets of his jacket. I gladly did so, noting how solid it was, like the rest of Olaf, solid and safe. Olaf—a rock one could cling to. But then, did one really *want* to be a frail creature clinging to a rock?

We walked along the street, looking at the shop windows and not saying much. It was much more fun browsing this way than alone. I didn't mind not buying, nor did I think about how little I could afford. I was happy for the companionship.

After that we strolled around the canal, Olaf admiring the boats and me nodding my head, not having much to add to the nautical conversation.

It was damp here by the edge of the canal. Olaf leaned over the railing and peered down at the water. I joined him. There was nothing much to see, only the choppy stream being endlessly confronted and frustrated by the dead end wall.

Olaf moved closer to me, so that the sleeves of our coats touched. I leant on the railing with my forearms crossed. Olaf placed my hand in his palm and examined it, as if he were cradling a delicate leaf.

"Such a small hand," he said, then let it go.

"I'm a small person."

I stared at my hand because I felt too shy to look at Olaf. His touch had startled me, all the more because it had felt so nice and had caused a burning sensation in me, not unlike the warm intense feeling of the liqueur, shooting downwards. It had been so long since anyone had touched me that way.

"Not so small," he argued.

"Are you happy?" he asked me, suddenly switching course.

I looked up again at his questioning face.

"Happy? I guess so. I'm not unhappy." I answered soundly enough then wondered about my conviction.

"Are you?" I asked, sensing that it was probably his own happiness that concerned him.

"I am *very* happy – except for one thing: I want to marry. I want a family. I almost married once, and then... I've been alone for a while now. And you? Do you want to be married?"

"Married?"

It should have been a simple question. For any other young woman I imagined it would have been. For most other young women, I imagined further, the answer would have been simple, too: yes. For me, it was only another problem question, which, like a tidal wave, tossed me about, heaving me up and down on the stormy sea of the unanswered questions of my life. This one confused me more than I realized. I had not given much serious consideration to this question and when, in a fit of social consciousness, I did think about it I would experience unarticulated, uncomfortable misgivings that I didn't understand myself, so how could I begin to explain it to this stranger?

The best I could do was to mutter "Oh, I don't know," which was as honest as anything, and then, before I could stop myself I blurted, "Why don't you marry Elizabeth?"

Olaf pulled at his beard and laughed. "Elizabeth?" he said, and laughed again, as if it were the most absurd idea he had ever heard. "She is like a sister. Would I marry my sister? No, no. We're just friends. I don't love her that way."

"I'm sorry," I said. "I don't know why I said that.

"Because you are a kind person."

I was terribly chilled now, standing by the water in the diminishing winter afternoon, and I asked Olaf if we could go.

"Come," he said, wrapping his thickly-coated arm around me and steering me away from the canal. "Let's go home." Olaf's casual self-confidence astonished me. How did he know that I would go home with him so obligingly? But, of course, he was right, yet again. I just smiled at him, let him take me to the street, let him hold me close to him while we waited for a cab, and let him caress my hands the entire ride back to his place.

As I expected, Olaf had a beautiful apartment in a middle class suburb of the city. Old brick row houses sported well kept lawns and window boxes, now bereft of their flowers, and, leading up to every front door, narrow little sidewalks that were outlined in low, neatly trimmed shrubbery.

Olaf lived on the top floor of one of these, in a large one bedroom apartment with tall ceilings and a skylight in the pitched roof of a vast living room where a deep red oriental carpet was framed by a highly polished wood floor. Olaf was proud of the skylight, which he bragged about having installed himself with the consent of the landlord. It made a wonderful shower of light, which was always needed in this overcast city, but also for his abundant plants, hanging and potted, large and small, especially one tall bushy tree by the window that faced the street. I had anticipated more paintings on the walls, but there were only a few large posters, a few advertising graphics, also large, and some modern abstract reproductions that were not familiar to me, probably Scandinavian painters.

Olaf told me to sit down, and I fell into the corner of a deep, plush sofa while he disappeared. He came back in a few minutes carrying two thin-stemmed, rosebud-like glasses of white wine. I was just recovering from the Cherry Heering and, therefore, dismayed at the prospect of slipping into an inebriated state again, but I was pliant now and wanted to please him, so I accepted the wine with no argument and a polite thank you.

Olaf sat in the large reclining easy chair next to me and sipped his wine. He returned the glass to the wooden coffee table at his feet and lay back in the chair, which made a mechanical thump, placed his arms behind his head and stared at me.

Oddly enough, this did not make me feel self-conscious. I smiled at him and stared at his reclining body, which was probably the purpose of this pose. So, Olaf did have his manipulations. This amused me, although it seemed slightly out of character for him. The angle of the recliner pushed his pelvis upwards and one could hardly not notice the bulging form straining against his pants. He was very appealing in this position, if only his relaxed and open attitude.

"Is the wine O.K.?" he asked, noting that I had put my glass on the table and hadn't picked it up again.

"Oh, yes," I said, retrieving it and taking a sip.

"Did you do those?" I asked, pointing to the advertising posters with my wine glass, one for a car and the other for a brand of gin or vodka.

This made Olaf sit up in his chair and he started to tell me about the posters, how he had done the artwork and the design of it, the lettering, etc. and in the middle of this explanation joined me on the sofa. I complimented him on his work and on his apartment and furnishings.

"Thank you," he said, then kissed me.

I kissed him back.

We tacitly agreed to continue kissing. Our ardent kissing grew more ardent and we collapsed into the sofa.

Olaf, now more consistent with his personality, had the ability to be passionate with a controlled sensitivity that I had never experienced before. He felt me without groping, was gentle without being hesitant and did not force his body on me but rather gracefully pulled me towards him and moved himself against me in a way that I can only describe as inviting. He suddenly stood up and took my hand. "Come." He led me into the bedroom with the same casual grace with which he had led me everywhere else that day.

The wineglasses remained abandoned where we left them, three-quarters empty after a final sip, at one end of the coffee table. The two fragile sentinels stood guard there for the rest of the afternoon, but over what I do not know.

Afterwards, we both fell asleep. I woke up first. Of course Olaf would have a way of sleeping that was as aesthetic as everything else he did: one arm over his head, the other on his leg, one leg straight and one slightly bent underneath it. He had beautiful legs—long, thin, and muscular.

As I admired his sleeping body I began to feel myself being pulled downward, my heart a dimming sun quickly sinking below the horizon. It was a common feeling I had after sex. I did not understand this feeling and usually brushed it aside, washed it off in the shower as I washed off the secretions, and forgot about it by the time I was dry.

That afternoon, watching Olaf sleep, I was not moved to shower, although the bathroom door opened onto the bedroom, and I could see the tub from my side of the bed. I didn't have a change of clothing, I rationalized, and the heavy feeling immobilized me. It felt worse than usual precisely because I told myself that I should have felt so good. I should have been elated or blissful, at the very least satisfied. I felt none of these things. Instead, I felt only a sense of hollowness inside a body of molded skin and bones.

Olaf woke up shortly and I suddenly felt the need to wrap the sheet around me tightly, as if I were cold. Without speaking he covered me with the down comforter and left to shower. I was dressed by the time he finished. He tried to persuade me to stay for coffee, but I insisted that it was late, that I wanted to get back.

On my way out he covered my face with kisses, still wrapped in his towel and smelling of soap, and only let me go after I promised to see him again, which I was not sure I wanted to do, but I could not bring myself to disappoint him, not just then.

I sat in the back of the cab, slumped in the corner on the passenger side with my head against the padded window frame, staring at the toes of my boots, which I dug into the shabby carpet. The old seat upholstery also was in bad shape, faded and torn in a few places. Though dusk had cast a pall over the city, I reminded myself that it had been a perfectly lovely day. I had been wined, dined and charmed. Now the wine had worn off, the food had been digested, and Olaf's charm had tarnished. I had been sexually satisfied, I argued further, hadn't I? Then, had I? *Had* I? It was a question that bobbed out of the depths as I was transported in the early evening gloom through the flat, winding Copenhagen streets, a question that I pushed down again before I faced the womb-pink walls of Hotel Blumendahl.

Chapter 8

Elke. What was she doing there, standing behind the glass door, like a mannequin posed in a store window, just as I stepped out of the elevator? As if she knew I was arriving then, as if she had been waiting for me?

She opened the door and beamed at me in her cheerful blond way. "Good evening."

"Good evening," I said brusquely and hurried down the hall to my room, passing Manfred. My door key didn't work, and I had to fiddle with the lock. Manfred watched me struggle with it, then offered to help.

"There," he said, letting me in.

I possessed an apparent inability to open doors for myself in that place. Manfred blocked the doorway so that I couldn't close it either.

"Ja, wait, I forgot this one." He picked up the loaded plastic straw wastebasket filled with my refuse under the sink.

I insisted that it wasn't important and he insisted on emptying it for me. Really. The wastebasket.

While he did this, my door still open, I removed my coat and shoes. I was dying for a shower and a change of clothes. Manfred took his time but finally came back not only with the empty basket but a fresh stack of towels, which was hardly necessary since clean towels were clearly hanging folded neatly as napkins on the metal rack.

"Here, you have these extra towels," he said, holding them flat in his hands before me, like a sacred offering.

I thanked him and made a move to close the door. Manfred retreated slowly and smiled at me before he left, pulling the door shut.

Alone. Finally. Behind the door. Away from leering, questioning, admiring eyes. I practically tore my clothes off; I was so anxious to be cleansed.

I ran down the hall in my bathrobe, bolted the bathroom door, and plunged into the shower without even bothering to check the temperature of the water. Fortunately it was hot right away, and I stood letting the waterfall pour over me for a long time before I reached for the soap. Then I scrubbed my body with the thickest lather I could make until I was convinced that I had shed one layer of skin.

No sooner had I showered and changed in my room than Elke knocked on the door, asking me to join her for coffee. She had just made a pot.

I knew that a refusal would only elicit a polite but energetic argument from Elke, and I felt renewed now. Fresh coffee would suit the moment.

I opened the door, and greeted Elke's sunshine face again.

"How pretty," she said, eyeing my new pants and sweater outfit as we walked side by side to the lounge.

"Thank you."

"And very flattering."

I opened my mouth to speak again but Elke's questioning stare stopped me.

"Why are you thanking me? I only told you what I thought."

"Just being polite. Don't you usually thank someone when they give you a compliment?"

"Of course not. Not here we don't. Ah, I see. This must be something American. Such an American girl." She nodded her head, agreeing with herself.

Elke wanted to sit on the "divan", so we each sat at one end, where there were little folding café tables, on which to rest our coffee cups. The "divan" was actually a small, rather hard and threadbare loveseat covered in a dull brick colored upholstery fabric at the far end of the breakfast room. It faced a portly old wooden TV console, which was crowned with a new bouquet of plastic flowers in a ceramic bowl that floated in a round pool of lace. There was no rug to warm the cold, sickly beige tiled floor, and I longed for some pillows to lean against to soften the couch. Two matching easy chairs mirrored each other on either side of the TV, whose grim, charcoal face stared blankly at us.

Elke flicked off her loafers and tucked her legs under

her skirt, curling into the corner of the sofa like a large housecat.

I kept my shoes on and sat upright, my legs crossed.

"Ah, it is good to sit down," Elke said. "All day I have been cleaning and changing the beds."

She leaned her head against the sofa and turned towards me in such a way that I expected her to put the back of her hand melodramatically against her forehead and sigh.

She did look rather tired. I believed she wasn't merely posing. If so, she was a very good actress. I never knew how much to believe with Elke, she being always so hyperbolic. Every movement, every remark was followed by an exclamation point.

"Good coffee," I said, raising my cup to her before replacing it on the saucer.

"I always buy fresh. I must treat my guests good. Everyone who stays at our hotel should be happy." Elke said this emphatically, as if she had been an innkeeper for many years, rather than merely one week.

"Of course, people must be happy. Otherwise they'll leave, go to the next place."

Elke sat up straighter, leaned towards me and stared at me hard. "Are you happy here?"

"Oh, yes. It's fine," I answered simply, though, as usual when Elke asked me a question, I felt it as a harpoon thrust to spear me and haul me into shore.

She sat back again, nodding her head with a self-satisfied smile.

"And you? What did you do today? You also look tired."

Now that she mentioned it, I did feel tired, although I hadn't noticed it until then, when I was finally still.

"Nothing much—some window shopping. I had lunch in Nyhavn."

"Nyhavn? You had lunch with the fishermen?" Elke chuckled at this for some indiscernible reason. Then she got up to pour herself another cup of coffee.

"More?" she asked me from the table.

I replied that I wasn't ready for more, thank you, and what was so funny about Nyhavn?

"Nothing," she said, sitting down and again folding herself into a tight ball, hugging her knees close to her chest and eyeing me over her kneecaps.

Blue eyes peered at me.

"You look different tonight."

"It must be my clothes. They're new."

"It's *not* the clothes."

Exclamation point.

I held my cup to my lips and drank as nonchalantly as I could in front of those scrutinizing eyes.

"I don't know." I shrugged.

She maintained this pose, scanning me like a searchlight.

"Ah, you are keeping a secret. You have so many secrets. You are always hiding things."

I must have looked guiltier than I thought. I, contrary

to Elke, was a very bad actress, and, obviously, a very bad liar. If I was always hiding things, I was also hiding them from myself.

"No secrets," I said.

She shook her head and smiled.

She let go of her knees and stretched out her legs, so that her socks grazed my thigh. I inched over to give her some room, making me feel cornered in the loveseat.

"Why did you buy this place?" I asked, thinking of secrets. "And where are the Blumendahls?"

"Oh, the Blumendahls. Such sweet people. They are old now. They went to the country. To the seaside. To rest."

"You mean they retired?"

"Retired. Yes. I was working in the office and I wanted to work for myself, *we* wanted to work for ourselves, together. Manfred knows money, I know people. So it is perfect for us."

I tried to imagine the Blumendahls in their seaside retirement cottage, but it was a hazy image. Their disappearance felt more foreboding, more like the plot of The Two. The Two didn't acquire the hotel, they descended upon it. And Elke knew people? She certainly wasn't shy.

Poor Elke. I was being so hard on her. Then again, she was so hard on me. I didn't understand what I had done to elicit her teasing scorn. I also wasn't sure if she was being scornful or merely trying to provoke me for reasons I couldn't fathom.

"Yes, I see," I said, finally.

I sat back and watched her stretched-out cat body that curved into the loveseat as I drank the freshly made, very delicious coffee. Perhaps it was the aroma that bewitched me, but I couldn't stop myself from admiring Elke, in spite of her strangeness. There was a certain grace about her, an easiness that was likeable. Then her perfect face—straight delicate nose, high cheekbones, full pink mouth, pale smooth skin, those searing blue eyes and thick eyebrows, yellow straight blond hair thinly poured over her head and shoulders, and that eternally balmy and endless smile that expressed so much in its variations but never turned downwards. I admired her, like a pretty picture that I could have placed on the wall and watched for hours. It certainly would have been an improvement over the dour print of a still life in my room.

I told her that I wanted another cup of coffee and she, of course, began to rise, but I stopped her and insisted on getting it myself. I wanted her to stay where she was and continue to look soft and supple. Elke should have always reposed in that curled position. It took the edge off her.

This time I sat in the armchair and faced Elke.

She squinted at me, as if I cast a too bright light.

"You are tired. Tomorrow you should rest."

"Maybe."

"*I* will rest tomorrow."

"You should. You worked hard today."

"I love to work hard." Her eyes dilated to their fullest. "It is good to work, isn't it?"

I silently disagreed with her as I didn't genuinely share this enthusiasm for work, probably because, as Olaf had put it, my "living" was still a mystery to me.

"You must find something that you love. Then you will love working hard," Elke said in her habitually clair-voyant way.

She took a long sip of coffee and let out a great sigh.

"You must think of it like love," she continued. "When you find someone to love, someone you love with all of your heart, then you will love them very hard, and no amount of loving will seem too much."

"I suppose," I said, wondering how and when I would find someone and something to love. I was also troubled by Elke's uncanny ability to read my thoughts. Was I that transparent, with no armor?

The chair became uncomfortable. I wanted to stretch my legs and move around. I couldn't respond to Elke's philosophy of love. I had never loved anyone or anything as she had described it and wasn't sure if this was true or not. I crossed my right leg over my left and sank back deeper into the cushions.

Manfred entered just then and settled himself heavily into the opposite armchair. All his gestures carried this weight, even the nod he gave me, how he bent his head slightly to the side when he did this, and his bulging lips that widened at the same moment in the same ponderous sort of way.

Manfred gave me a perfect reason to retreat. I felt

outnumbered by The Two, who together were more than I could handle. Manfred baldly stared at me, with his watery bullish eyes. He was rude this way, a rudeness that knew no self-consciousness.

I excused myself, pleading hunger and the need to make it an early evening. They both waved at me, broad smiles on their faces, as I backed out of the room, wishing them to "have a good evening."

What a surprise to find *The Couple In The Window* when I approached the curtains. I hadn't seen them in days. It was shocking to suddenly see them now, sitting in their living room, reading newspapers together in matching wing chairs by the fireplace. I felt guilty about watching, as if I had caught them in a more pernicious act. Really, reading newspapers. How mundane, how boring, how perfectly innocuous. And fascinating. Again, I couldn't help being captivated by their ordinariness. They weren't even looking at each other or talking, merely reading and turning the pages. How could they be so positively placid and look so content? Couldn't they do something wild, just once? I kept staring at them as I slowly pulled the drapes and ended their scene.

I was truly hungry and needed to think about dinner. Restaurant hunting had become a routine that made me feel primitive. I was not a traveler seeking a meal; I was a native foraging for food in the wilderness. It was a primal rite, like mating.

I thought about this in some depth as I gathered my

coat, gloves, and bag. I didn't understand the mating ritual, either. Each tribe had its own. For example, Elke belonged to one, Elizabeth to one, Olaf to his, and *The Couple In The Window* to yet another. Not only did I not understand the rituals. I wasn't sure to which tribe I belonged.

I ate dinner at a small café nearby and then thought about returning to the club, but the possibility of accidentally running into Olaf sent me back to the hotel. I settled for an early evening, making my white lie the truth.

After being out in the cold night, I was happy to be warm again in the narrow bed. I sat up and read for a while, from a paperback I had bought for such an emergency, about a man who had lived with and studied a pack of wolves in the Canadian wilderness.

I remember the passage I read just before I fell asleep: the man had been stalking the wolves all day, lying on his stomach on a concealing rock for hours, binoculars glued to his eyes, searching for but not seeing any wolves. When he finally stood up and turned around to relieve himself, he faced a pair of wolves reclining on their bellies, who, all the while, had been watching him.

Chapter 9

Yin and Yang sat side by side at the table with the yellow floral oilcloth, eating the continental breakfast.

Yin was Elke, of course, the white witch, a look this morning accentuated by her habitual monotones, this time a fleecy white sweater and skirt. But who was Yang? A dark-haired, dark-skinned, dark-eyed Medusa. She even dressed darkly—a heavy wool shirt and brown corduroys, the same color as her deep-set brown eyes that reminded me of the glassy opaque eyes on a stuffed animal. Her thick, straight bangs merged with a nearly continuous line of eyebrow, and her hair hung loose and straight as a plumb line and perpendicular to the point where her neck met her shoulders, all of which gave her the effect of wearing a medieval helmet.

Elke was happy to see me and invited me to join them across the table.

"This is my friend, Margarethe," she said, smiling at Margarethe, then at me.

"Pleased to meet you," I said, sitting down.

Margarethe the Yang didn't return the greeting, nor did she smile. Instead, she gave me an allover dubious look that was less than cordial and snorted like an impatient horse.

Elke poured coffee into my cup, graciously distracting me from Margarethe, who meanwhile, to my relief, had renewed her interest in a breakfast roll. Strong coffee and rudeness were an arousing mixture of ingredients that woke me up, to say the least. Her rudeness had only stimulated my curiosity. Who was this woman, and why did she take such an instant dislike to me? Why was this hard-looking woman Elke's friend, of all people?

I would find out. My attitude suited my adventurous mood that morning, for I had decided on waking that I would try to find Elizabeth.

"How do you know Elke?" I asked boldly, tackling disdain with inquisitiveness.

Surprised by my directness, Margarethe looked at me then questioningly at Elke, who ignored her and sipped coffee, eyes focused on the contents of the cup. Margarethe clearly did not want to tell me this or anything else.

"We were at the office. I have a different job now."

"That's good," I said, acknowledging what I assumed to be a dead-end conversation.

"Not really. It's not very good. No job is very good here. One is as bad as the next. You work, work, work and they take all your money. Taxes. The welfare state. Hah.

Not my welfare."

She tore a long strip off the roll and stuffed it in her mouth.

"But you have all those benefits: education, medical care..."

"Oh, sure. It's fine if you go to university or you're sick. What if you don't go to university or you're not sick? You still have to pay. You pay for everyone else to go to university and be sick. Taxes, taxes, taxes. And no money. You can go to university. I want some money. I'm not the one traveling in your country."

Just then one of the boarders, the short one, entered and poured himself a cup of coffee, which he took with a mound of breakfast rolls on a small plate to the opposite table. On his way he had given Margarethe, then me, the once-over, ending the awkward conversation.

All this time Elke had been uncharacteristically silent. I had never seen her take a backseat to anyone, certainly not to Manfred. Margarethe's presence diminished Elke, her darkness transforming Elke's usual sparkle into a faint light. Elke's expression towards me was equally limp. I couldn't fathom this unusual change in attitude, an aberration in her personality that confused me all the further about Elke, who, the more I saw of her, the less I understood. I didn't know how to respond to Margarethe. Her rampage against the political structure stunned me. I had never heard such an attack on the social welfare system. In my naive imaginings, I thought of the Scandinavians

as a society of contented, well-cared-for sheep happily
following the shepherd of the welfare state. To think that
anyone would dare to reject and rail against such a humane
and civilized social order disturbed my equilibrium. I had
to agree that Margarethe's arguments made good sense,
but I could not reconcile the conflict she had described.
Having no personal experience of the welfare state but
having a blind faith in its efficacy, I concluded that the
problem must lie within Margarethe, who, I sensed,
would continue to disperse her shadows around the
table. She resented my presence there as intensely as Elke
welcomed it, which threw me into a deeper confusion.
Clearly, I had yet to understand the Danes, a species that
I continued to observe through the dim binoculars of my
consciousness.

"And what are you doing today?" Elke asked me.

"Nothing much. I'll figure it out when I get there, I
suppose."

In fact, I knew exactly what I was doing: I was going
to Christianshavn, to hunt for Elizabeth. What made me
think I could find her I don't know, but I was as determined and confident as any experienced tracker. Such was
my innocent bravado in those days and my passionate need
to add another souvenir life experience to my baggage.

Margarethe smirked at me. I don't think I had ever felt
more uncomfortable in someone else's presence.

"I really think you should rest today," Elke said.
"Remember how tired you were yesterday."

I shrugged.

"It's not a good day—so cold. You can come to dinner with me and Margarethe. We will go out later."

Besides my complete disinterest in this plan, I noticed the alarm in Margarethe's face and quickly declined, insisting that I needed to go out. But she was right, it was a lousy day, dreary and cold. The breakfast room was dark at mid-morning. The murky light accentuated our grim party, and I was actually relieved, for once, when Manfred sat down with us and squared off our unhappy triangle.

Manfred was mute, as usual. He rarely spoke, even to Elke, and when he did it was brief. I never knew what to say to him. There was a basic lack of communication between us that went beyond the language barrier. It wasn't his English, which was clear. Mr. Blumendahl, who spoke little English, and I had had a much better rapport. Through the shared gropings of gesture, feeling and facial expression, we understood one another perfectly and communicated a genuine mutual sense of appreciation. The problem with Manfred was that he did communicate something to me, something that I didn't want to know, so I backed away from it.

He spoke in Danish, first to Margarethe then to Elke, and I was left out of the conversation. There is no more truly descriptive phrase than "the language barrier". How I wished I could climb over that wall. What were they talking about that they should choose to discuss it in Danish, excluding me? Everything sounds so much more compelling and important in an unknown foreign language. They could have been discussing the weather or their plans for the day, for all I knew. Or me.

This last possibility struck me when they suddenly switched to English and turned their attention to me.

Manfred placed his hand on the back of my chair and leaned closely towards me, smothering me with his pungent cologne that smelled like dry, musty leather.

"You will go out today? It's not good. Stay here with us. We will have a nice lunch. We won't charge you. We would like you to stay."

He said this gently and sincerely enough, but I wasn't moved.

The more this plan was suggested to me the less appealing it became—a whole day with Elke, Manfred and now the hateful Yang? I couldn't conceive of it. Of course, I thanked him and politely declined, assuring them all that I had plans and in fact I should be going, it was getting late.

When I rose from my chair, Margarethe finally smiled at me, and waved goodbye with the rest of them.

I knew I could count on the Reliable Prince to give me the right directions to Christinshavn. Without bothering to consult *No Dollars*, I proceeded to Rådhuspladsen where I found the very tall sign for the #17 bus, which indicated that it did, indeed, take one to Christianshavn. The square was bereft of people now, owing probably to the fact that it was Sunday and dismal. I was the only one at the bus stop in contrast to the day before when so many pedestrians were crossing and criss-crossing the square that I could barely see to the other side. The big, silent, sculpture fountain was conspicuously drained of its water for the winter.

The complete absurdity of what I was about to attempt never occurred to me, only its inevitable success. I felt an urgent need to find Elizabeth. I must find her. I didn't question my motives. I believed I had no motives. I was seeking an adventure, a real one this time, with the Mystery, the Quest, and the Discovery that an adventure required.

The bus was nowhere in sight, nor did I notice any of the other buses at any of the other bus stops around the square, nor potential passengers waiting for them. I was beginning to wonder if the buses perhaps didn't run on Sunday, something I had neglected to investigate in the guidebook. However, soon a young man in a rather worn sheepskin coat walked over to me and stood two feet to my left, also waiting for the #17. He fished a pack of cigarettes from his large coat pocket and offered me one, the stubby European kind, which I refused. He lit one and puffed on it liberally. Gauzy, tattered clouds of smoke streamed by my face, scenting the air with the smell of strong, acrid tobacco.

I backed away from these ghosts, but they dogged me no matter which direction I chose, like stubborn shadows attached to my feet. I was glad to see the bus come if only to escape the ghosts, which, for the moment, had distracted me from my mission.

Christianshavn, apart from being one of Copenhagen's oldest neighborhoods, was also one of the city's many islands. Copenhagen is a city of islands in a country of islands, an unconnected puzzle of a landscape, with numerous scattered pieces bound by water. I was often baffled by the terrain and confused about the direction in which I was going, as I navigate poorly on water.

We crossed the bridge that linked Christianshavn to the island on which the square stood. I expected to see a much quainter scene, but it was not picturesque, merely old and tired. Now I understood why the bus was so unpopulated. Only an elderly woman with some parcels in white bags was on the bus and another young man. I boarded first and the smoker took a seat in the back. I had chosen a seat in the front, nervous about missing the stop.

I studied my section map of Christianshavn and looked for a street that began with the letters on the scrap of paper I had kept with Olaf's writing, which I now held tightly in my hand. The neighborhood was relatively small, and I could easily read every street name on the map. I was pleasantly surprised to discover that there was only one street beginning with the letter "B". I was further assured that since this was also the last stop, at least I wouldn't miss it, which for a while seemed a likely probability since the streets looked so similar, with low, stone row houses, only a few small cars parked here and there. I don't believe I saw one person. When we arrived at the end of the line the driver looked at me as if to say "this is it". I had been the only passenger for the last ten minutes of the ride. In fact, the road ended here and the bus had to turn itself completely around.

I may as well have been in the middle of the tundra. There was no greenery, no trees or parks on the route the bus had taken, simply deserted, drab streets of dark gray stone. There were no pretty lawns or window boxes on Elizabeth's street, as in Olaf's neighborhood, only the sad faces of old stone row houses that had weathered the damp winds of many winters.

I stared and stared down the narrow street, but no life emerged. Looking at the uninterrupted row of four-story apartment houses, I pondered what to do next. The street was so quiet, I imagined that I could hear my heart beating.

I crossed the pavement to the first house and stood on the narrow sidewalk looking across the street and back again, trying to devise a plan for deciphering the indecipherable. The buildings on both sides of the street were identical, as if reflected by a mirror, and any one of them could have been Elizabeth's.

My plan was quite simple: to go up one side of the street and down the other. This may not have been the most efficient plan but it was certainly practical to my way of thinking, and it was infinitely more appealing than returning to the hotel to face The Three.

As it turned out my plan was right, for when I opened the door of the first house I saw that there was a legend of the last names of the tenants in small brass plaques over the mailboxes. And to my astonishment there were large parent versions of these hung at midsection on every apartment door announcing who lived there, a practice that defied at least my own sense of logic. Was there no need for privacy? Clearly this was not a country in which to hide.

I checked the names on the mailboxes carefully, but as Elizabeth's was not one of them I stepped outside again and moved on to the next apartment house.

This building too had the same mailbox and door setup but Elizabeth's name didn't appear there either. I continued up the block, checking the names on all the mailboxes, which now strikes me as rather senseless, but then my quest was pressing, and on the seventh or eighth house I found my reward: a plaque with Elizabeth's last name. While this elated me at first, I hesitated. What would I say I was doing here? Surely one did not just pass through Christianshavn. I don't think I could have told her, and I hoped beyond reason that she wouldn't ask.

With cautious optimism I climbed the stairs to the first landing, but as her door wasn't here I continued to the second and found her finally on the fourth, where the initial "E" was also on the plaque, so there was no question of mistaken identities.

I knocked tentatively and a wan-looking Elizabeth cracked the door open slightly to see who it was. Her face grew even paler when she recognized me.

"Oh," she said, sucking in her breath in surprise. Then she opened the door wider and asked me to come in. She looked both puzzled and disturbed by my presence.

"How did you find me? You shouldn't see this place. It's so..." She waved her arm from one end of the room to the other.

In one quick glance I could see that the apartment was small, that the dingy white walls were in dire need of painting, that she owned little, and that what she had was second-hand and shabby. The door opened into a small living room with a kitchen in an alcove to my left. I assumed the bedroom was behind the kitchen down the short hallway.

"How are you?" I asked. She looked like she had just woken up, perhaps with a hangover.

She smiled at me in a tired kind of way. "I'm good. It's good to see you. Sit down. I told Olaf not to tell–

"He didn't tell me your address. He only started to and wrote down the first few letters of the street. I found the street and then I found your building."

I was sitting in a well worn and overstuffed easy chair. Elizabeth had taken a seat in the corner of a small sofa. She was wearing ski pants and a long turtleneck the color of medium toast that brought out her dark innocent eyes and warmed her pale skin.

"You found me? This is...is...I don't know how to say it in English—more than I can understand, more than is possible. You are such a special girl. I knew you were. I was telling Olaf you are so much like me, a girl on her own and not afraid to do what she is not supposed to do—go to a strange country all alone, not afraid what people think. I tell you I am the same. I don't have to be the girl everyone wants me to be. I write poems, I don't have any children. I won't be the wife of the farmer and making the butter. You found me. I must tell this to Olaf."

"Olaf found me yesterday," I blurted out before I realized that it was perhaps a subject on which I did not want to elaborate.

"Olaf? Where?"

"At Rådhuspladsen."

"Rådhuspladsen?" The animation left Elizabeth's face. "Oh no, I forgot to meet you. I am so sorry for this. You will think I am a terrible person."

"It's all right. Don't worry about it. I had lunch with Olaf in Nyhavn. I had a very nice day, really." Elizabeth looked at me as if she was about to ask me more about my afternoon with Olaf but then thought better of it, and I was relieved when she dropped the subject. Olaf would be forthcoming with her.

Elizabeth glanced at her watch. "Ah, we don't have too much time. Kurt will be here in one half hour. We are going to the country to get a table for me. You see I have no table to eat on. There is a table in his parents' house in the north by the sea. Four of us are going but there is room in the big car. You will come with us? Please come, it will be much better than meeting in Rådhuspladsen. I would like it. Yes?"

"Who's Kurt, and the others...?"

"Kurt is my ex-husband, of course. Then his girl-friend, Else, and Else's ex-husband Hans. Everyone else's everyone else. It is all very friendly."

Elizabeth gave me a wide-eyed smile.

"You must be kidding. Your ex-husband, his girlfriend and her ex-husband, to get a table?"

"Yes, to get a table. It is a very pretty ride to the north, just past Elsinore," she added, referring to the famous castle, as if that was a perfectly logical explanation for why this group should travel together.

The more Elizabeth talked about this trip, the more amused she became and the more misgivings I had: maybe I shouldn't be in the middle of this disparate party. Did I really want to meet these people? This might be the kind of adventure that I hadn't bargained for. But now that I was in Elizabeth's presence I couldn't leave. I wanted to be with her, I wanted to know her.

Elizabeth intrigued me; she was everything that I wanted to be–independent, free, easy-going–and she liked me; she said I was already like her. This was enormously flattering to me, more than she could know.

"You will come?"

"Sure, why not. It should be fun."

"This is good. It will make right for yesterday. I told Kurt about you. He will like to meet you. He likes girls like you–just not to marry them!"

She released a sardonic chuckle, which was more like a cough. Her acceptance of these rearranged couplings puzzled me, but I had some sort of answer in that choked laugh.

She excused herself to get ready and disappeared down the hallway. I surveyed Elizabeth's apartment again. I saw the packed bookshelves, two large cases of well-used books. This intellectual rigor made up for the dearth of furnishings and the cold floor with only a tiny rectangle for a carpet. What were those books? With what did she feed that strong labyrinthine mind? Of all the unfathomable Danes I had met so far, Elizabeth was the one I understood the least and yet she was the one I liked the most. I couldn't say why. She was right somehow about us being "the same girl". I did not question my responses. I only knew I was content being there.

I began to relax now. This would be quite an adventure, and thoroughly amusing. I was relieved that Elizabeth wasn't mad at me for my intrusion and that both of us wanted to forget the day before.

Elizabeth returned, having replaced her bare feet in flats with warm socks and ankle boots that tied up the front with spaghetti-thin laces. She had also brushed her hair and put on an oversized, thick, snow-white cardigan. I thought she looked wonderful, but I felt too shy to tell her. She sat down again and looked at her watch.

"Kurt should be here. Are you hungry? We will have some lunch when we go. There is a place we like in the country. Oh, I am so happy you are coming."

"So am I."

Elizabeth smiled at me, but this time without any cynicism.

I smiled back, staring into her large blue eyes. There was a knock at the door.

Chapter 10

Still smiling, Elizabeth answered the door. I heard an exchange in Danish then a short dark-haired man with a close-clipped beard entered the room. He saw me and blinked as if I had just taken his picture with a flash camera.

"This is Kurt," Elizabeth said.

This time he smiled, blinked and shook my hand all at once. It turned out that he had the kind of eyes that blinked a lot, small bittersweet chocolate eyes. Perhaps it was the long, thick lashes that weighed down the lids.

"Where is Else?" Elizabeth asked in English.

"She is waiting in the car," he said in reverent tones.

"You are coming with us?" Kurt asked me, although Elizabeth surely had just told him so.

"If that's O.K.–"

"Of course it is O.K.," Elizabeth said to Kurt.

"Of course," he said. "Plenty of room."

"Plenty of room," Elizabeth repeated. "Come now, Else is waiting."

She smiled and winked at me behind Kurt's back, screwing her mouth up to one side in such a comical way that I almost laughed out loud and Elizabeth, too.

I followed them down the narrow, barely lit stairs. I couldn't help but think that this would be a bizarre trip, but what the hell. Actually, I liked Kurt, that is, what I had seen of him so far. A quiet and serious man, he had a pensive, introspective look. He was not unlike Elizabeth in that respect. His smile was restrained but genuine. However, I couldn't see him joining us at the club. I couldn't imagine him drunk. He would have listened to the music and said thoughtful things about it, and nodded his head and blinked a lot.

The car was an old station wagon with oak and blond wooden siding, a local make I had never seen that was, indeed, enormous. It would easily accommodate five people and a table.

Else gave us a cherubic smile through the open window, nonplused by my presence. Kurt introduced us and she enthusiastically said "hello" to me and then gave a "hi" to Elizabeth in English and kissed her cheek. Elizabeth received this graciously, which was beyond bewildering to me.

Else was the antithesis of Kurt and Elizabeth—a beauty with a round face and ski slope nose, typically flaxen but curly Scandinavian blond hair slightly below her shoulders that bounced this way and that every time she turned her head, which was often.

As the car quickly sped us away from Christianshavn, Else turned around and spoke to Elizabeth, in Danish mostly. English was a strain for her. And even though I couldn't understand a word of her conversation, I knew that it was either chit-chit, insubstantial musings, or gossip, from the light musical tone of her voice and intermittent giggles, a not unpleasant sound, but also not a melody that would linger in one's mind or touch one deeply.

Kurt's bass answers would interrupt Else's bell-like tones every once in a while. Elizabeth struck a balance between them, like a violin with the lead part. And I became the captive audience to this private grand performance, to which I had been invited.

I sat by the back seat door on the passenger side and listened to the trio and their chamber music. I watched the city streets pass by, the neighborhoods becoming increasingly better the further we drove from Elizabeth's place. I noticed bigger and more beautiful homes with stone courtyards and tidy townhouses trimmed in sprawling shrubbery, though I was much more attuned to my fellow passengers and their indecipherable chimes.

We arrived at Hans's house in about twenty minutes, in a neighborhood not unlike Olaf's. The row houses here were probably late 19th century but modernized and well-kept. We parked in front of the house and everyone got out, except for Else, who waited expectantly for Kurt to open her door.

A beaming Hans greeted us in the doorway of his

second-story walk-up apartment. He hugged Else, gave Kurt's hand a vigorous shake, kissed Elizabeth on the cheek, and shook my hand more gently than Kurt's. A tall, lanky man with shaggy blond hair, he wore gold wire-rimmed glasses and professorial tweeds and corduroy. He was extremely happy to see everyone, a feeling they all returned. The atmosphere rained heavily with laughter and exuberance. I needed to remind myself that Hans was Else's ex-husband, a relationship about which one had to stretch the imagination quite a few miles.

We settled into Hans's tiny library-like living room, which was lined with built-in floor-to-ceiling shelves that were crammed with hardcover and paperback books. At the far end a shallow bay window with pale greenish/yellow colored glass corner panes cast a smoky amber mist across the room.

Hans sank into an upholstered armchair. Elizabeth and Kurt, oddly enough, sat next to each other on the sofa, and Else and I ended up on the red oriental carpet near Hans, against an antique carved wooden blanket chest that was tucked into the corner against the wall.

The flat Danish sing-song started again, this time as a quartet, the laughing and talking often at the same time, overlapping and interrupting each other, until Elizabeth noticed the bewildered look on my face and said in English to Hans that this was my first trip to Denmark from America and "she is not understanding anything we say."

"Oh, excuse me," Hans said, turned to me and spoke

in a very clear English. "I thought you were one of us."

Without taking his eyes off me, he reached for a wood pipe that hung alone on a circular pipe rack on the end table next to his chair under the wide umbrella of a leaded glass lampshade. He fished in his jacket pocket for a pouch of tobacco, which he held in one hand while filling the pipe with his other, a studied and efficient gesture that I observed with some fascination.

"So, you're traveling," he said, with burning cool eyes, the grey-blue color of dry ice. They didn't look at me. They seared me through the watery frozen lenses of his glasses and searched my face for the meaning of my life.

"Yes, a bit."

His eyes left me only for the few seconds it took him to strike a match and light the pipe. His tobacco was strong and bittersweet, rather like the pungent odor of burning oak leaves gathered from the fall clearing. I breathed in a gulp of its heady aroma.

"Hans is a translator," Elizabeth said suddenly, saving me from Hans's probing gaze.

Hans puffed harder on his pipe and crossed his left leg over his right.

"And he is a fine translator, too," Kurt said. He is translating the *I Ching* into Danish. T*he* official Danish edition."

"Only from the German." Hans took his pipe out of his mouth and pointed the stem at me an arm's length. "Of course I must refer to the original Chinese now and then."

The *I Ching* reminded me of a friend in college who was always throwing three Chinese coins like dice, drawing stacks of broken lines on paper, then telling me how my life was about to change in enormous and significant ways. The female lines changing to the male lines and all that, which mystified me.

Hans leaned back in his chair, content and relaxed, surely not in a hurry to go anywhere. In fact no one appeared to be going anywhere. As I looked around at us I couldn't help being reminded of a parlor scene in a Victorian play: a man posed regally in an easy chair, a man and a woman sitting closely together leaning back into a sofa, contrary to the true nature of their relationship, and two women, reclining languidly on an oriental carpet, at the feet of the regally sitting man who was smoking an elegant pipe. But there was something wrong with this picture: the arrangements were off, the groupings were unbalanced, the tone was false.

"Do you want to see our pictures?" Else asked, addressing everyone with a childlike gleefulness. "Hans, show them our pictures."

Ah, I thought to myself in confident tones, now the truth would be revealed. Hans would protest and there would be an ugly argument. The masks of cordiality would fall off their faces and lie at their feet on the swirling carpet, like the thin flaky dried skins of molting snakes.

"Yes, the pictures," Hans said jumping up, sharing Else's pleasure in them and none of my protest.

Hans hunted through the wall of bookshelves for the photo album. Kurt and Elizabeth shifted themselves to the edge of the sofa to be closer to us.

So much for the truth. I began to envy that man in the wilderness who had lived with the wolves. Although the animals were at first a mystery to him, eventually he began to understand them. They were consistent, they had certain habits, they did not express ambivalence or contradictions. He could learn his subject. I, however, seemed to know less the more I studied the human animal. In my youthful need for absolutes, I wanted The Answer. I wanted to know the hows and whys of love and desire, of coupling–and uncoupling. My subjects remained a mystery, however, and their mating habits continued to baffle me. On the other hand, those of the wolves were clear and simple: wolves mated for life.

Everyone huddled over the album. The photographs were not remarkable: vacations to Greece and Italy, skiing in Sweden, Else and Hans separately, Else and Hans together, Else with shorter hair, Hans with longer hair, Else on a picnic blanket with a small, fluffy white dog, both looking much younger and happier. Frozen in their snowy white snapshot frames, Else and Hans, with smiling faces and waving hands, would look happy forever. What was remarkable was this: that they had ever smiled together to begin with, and further, that one day they had stopped.

We left after the pictures and resumed our former positions in the car, only now Hans sat by the opposite door in back, so that Elizabeth was between us. I was glad for this, and not only because I liked being near Elizabeth. Hans's eyes frightened me. Elizabeth's eyes were large with understanding, Else's didn't focus too much, Kurt's pondered with a question. Hans's eyes, however, knew everything.

"I know you," they said. "I know everything about you. I know more about you than you know about yourself."

Suddenly we were in the countryside, a relief from the faces. I stared out the window at the passing wintry hills that rolled before me like breaking waves. They were a disappointment, those rolling waves of brown. I don't know what I expected in the middle of March—green pastures and frolicking villagers? To the contrary, in a very short time outside the city we passed little of note: barren fields and not a village to speak of, some isolated farmhouses here and there, an occasional church, tall white spires austerely protecting their invisible flocks. We were one of the few cars on the road. This wasn't surprising since there was not much to the north besides the tourist attraction of Elsinore castle and the sea, and we were out of season for both.

Nonetheless, I was mesmerized by the uneventful nothingness of the tame landscape, which was soothing in its plain regularity, its calming repetitious pattern, and now most welcome. My sensibilities had been disturbed by the juggling of partners and interpersonal relationships. This was yet the most foreign and jarring foreignness that I had discovered, and those gentle folds of brown earth were just the thing to ease my mind and draw me back into my sense of the normal.

The landscape had an effect on everyone else also. Soon the car was quiet as the others sat back and enjoyed the simple passing countryside. The road split the hills and stretched ahead into the horizon. Kurt drove at a conservative speed, though surely one could have flown on the deserted highway.

I felt comfortable staring out the window in a mindless reverie. Staring at anyone in the car would have been rude, and I didn't want to take the chance of encountering Hans. Once, I happened to turn my head and met Elizabeth's soulful eyes. She had a curious look on her face and smiled at me indulgently. She had clearly been observing me and not the scenes flashing across the window frames. I returned her smile but immediately retreated to the window, as I felt a blush coming on.

After an hour or so we stopped at a rustic inn for lunch. The plump proprietor welcomed us warmly and gave us a large table by a window. The place was quite empty and he acted delighted to see our large party. The inn was hundreds of years old, an establishment that one would expect to find in the Danish countryside. We sat at a rectangular table with a blue and white checkered cloth in dark wooden captain's chairs, each the captain of our own lonely ship.

Somehow I ended up sitting next to Hans, who was

closest to the window, with Else across from Hans in the other window seat, Kurt across from me, Elizabeth next to Kurt across from a sixth empty chair, the one unmatched set.

Hans's jacket smelled like his tobacco, with which he now filled his pipe since he had restrained himself from smoking in the car, quite politely I thought.

I decided it was silly of me to avoid him. He seemed nice enough. He had merely caught me off guard. I was even beginning to think he was handsome, in an austere, Scandinavian sort of way—those square cheekbones and cool eyes.

He smiled at me warmly.

I braved a smile at him.

"The food is good here," Hans said to me. "Do you like smørrebrød?"

"Oh, yes. Very much." And, as if I had cast the right spell, as I said this the food arrived and the table was filled with appetizing sandwiches and coffee.

Everyone dove into the food, eating and talking to each other with the same vehement passion. I, of course, was left out of the conversation again and was beginning to feel the loneliness of being lost in a crowd.

Hans persisted in watching me. He was listening to Kurt, but his eyes drifted over to me often. I turned to Elizabeth and tried not to catch them, although I could feel those icy beacons searing my back. I ate, intrigued by Elizabeth, who was very delicately cutting up her sandwiches into little squares and eating them European style with an upside down fork in the left hand and a knife in the right.

I had tried very hard to adopt this technique, which was so chic to me, but I soon gave up in hungry frustration as the food kept falling off the humpback of the fork and splattering onto my plate or my lap before it was halfway to my mouth. I admired Elizabeth's natural ease with her fork and knife. It was the same ease with which she accepted her disparate companions, and I wondered how she managed to balance the feelings that surely must have been evoked by their presence just as much as I wondered how she kept the slippery salads on the back of her fork.

I could not reconcile this picture of equanimity with her image only a few nights before—unbalanced, drunk— when she had merely spoken about Kurt and Else.

I could see from the corner of my eye that Hans continued to steal glances at me. Else talked and laughed, especially when Kurt responded to her, which encouraged her to talk and laugh at an ever increasingly high pitch.

"Do you want more?" Hans had picked up the plate of sandwiches on which there remained one herring salad and one perspiring smoked salmon on dark rye.

I protested with both hands.

He offered them to the others, who also declined, and then finished them both quickly himself. For such a thin man he had a voracious appetite and obviously loved to eat. His satiety showed in a Buddha-like grin.

Else giggled and said something to him after he had finished, at which he frowned.

"Do you know that we speak in accents?" Kurt asked me.

"Accents?"

"Yes, we are from different parts of the country, and, of course, Elizabeth is Swedish."

I assured him that accents were the last thing I would have noticed.

"Listen. We will each speak for you." He started and one by one they said a few sentences in their own brand of Danish. I could hear nothing to differentiate one from the other, so the demonstration was rather a flop, about which they were all disappointed.

"We *are* very different," Kurt insisted.

I wasn't convinced of this.

We lingered a while over coffee with shots of cognac, which I drank too quickly and on its way down felt like it was burning a hole through me, and then we were back on the road.

In no time, it seemed, we reached the town of Elsinore and, before I was prepared for it, the castle loomed ahead of us like a mountain that might suddenly appear around a bend in the road. Built on a square and fortress-like, its enormity and its impregnability were shocking. It could easily have contained a complete small town, which, in essence, it had been in its day. I watched it wide-eyed, but the others, benumbed by their familiarity with the castle, paid little attention to it.

Within minutes we arrived at a one-storey, roomy, old wooden house, which sat by the wide spacious beach behind it and the murky sea. The house was clearly closed up for winter, its wooden shutters fastened tight, and a large rusty padlock barred entrance to the front door.

It was wet and colder here but the sea air was a welcome change from the stuffy closet atmosphere of the car.

"Come, look at the sea." Hans wrapped an arm around me and lead me to the water. Over my shoulder I gave a wary glance to Elizabeth, who followed close behind us, her hands thrust into the depths of her pockets, her scarf hiked up over her ears.

No one made a move towards the house. Rather they all followed me and Hans and proceeded to stroll along the frigid beach.

"You are never far from the sea in Denmark," Hans said close to my ear. "Here all roads lead back to the sea."

We stood facing the water, and now, we too, burrowed our hands deep into the warmth of our pockets and pressed our arms close to our sides against the frozen breezes. The sky was a dark stone wall of mist. The afternoon light was gray, the kind of gray that is very revealing in its starkness. I had heard it said that a cloudy day is excellent for photographing because the light allows true color to be exposed, and I regretted not having brought my camera.

But then I had no idea where I would end up that day.

Elizabeth approached Hans and I, and the three of us walked on the sand precariously close to the water line. The water played tag with our feet and we had to dodge it every once in a while.

"On a clear day you can look across the water and see Sweden," Elizabeth said, pointing with her right hand, indicating northeast. "It's very close."

I looked and looked but couldn't see Sweden, couldn't see any land, nor could I see any sky, only the illusionary impenetrable fortress of mist and fog.

We decided to turn around and walk back. Kurt was far ahead of the rest, standing alone by the water's edge and gazing at the sea. Else kicked the sand with her feet every once in a while, casually beach combing. When she saw us approach, she waved her arm wildly. She called out to us in Danish to come look at something, but as I couldn't understand I asked Elizabeth to translate.

"A bird. A dead bird. I'll go see what it is."

Elizabeth ran ahead and left Hans and me to stroll at a leisurely pace.

When she was out of earshot, Hans said to me, "Why did you come here?"

"Elizabeth asked me this morn–"

"No, I mean why did you come to Denmark?"

"Oh, I don't know; I was curious I suppose."

"Curious about what?"

"You know, the open society and all that."

Hans arched his eyebrows. "And have you discovered the open society? What have you found?"

"Well...you know...people are friendly here," I said lightly, trying desperately to find my way out of this subject, which I now regretted mentioning. "They tell you what's on their minds. And I don't have to be afraid—at night."

"Afraid? Ah yes, so much crime in America." He made a disconcerting expression that meant, I don't believe a word you have said.

He was looking for something, but I didn't know what, and, once again I turned away from those probing eyes.

He fell silent for a minute as he fished for his pipe. We walked on as he packed and tried to light it, which took several attempts. He puffed on the pipe hard, and the smoke was quickly taken by the wind.

I was grateful for the silence. Kurt, Else and Elizabeth walked ahead of us, each at their own pace. I envied their solitude.

"Are you so afraid at home?" Hans asked suddenly.

"Sometimes one has to be careful." I had been staring at the water. My mind was more at sea than on land, so that I was startled when Kurt stopped walking, picked up my chin with his forefinger, and I was confronted with the burning aqua light of his eyes.

"One always must be careful. It is like the *I Ching* says—one has to find the balance in life and walk in the middle."

I didn't know whether he was getting at something or

just felt like philosophizing, and I was very happy when he released my chin.

We continued pacing the sand without speaking. His pipe had gone out, but he again managed to light it. This time the smoke blew in my face and smelled strangely sour in the salty air.

"The question is: why did you *really* come to Denmark, a young woman, alone, in the winter?"

"I already told you. Why do you keep asking me? Why do you care?"

In spite of the cold, I could feel the heat rising in my cheeks.

Hans shrugged. "I don't care. I see a look on your face, a look in your eyes. I like to know what things mean. That's my business."

We slowed our pace and walked quietly for a few minutes. Then Hans turned to me again.

"Perhaps you are running away from something?"

"Do you know that you are probably the nosiest person I have ever met?

"Well, are you?"

"Am I what?"

"Are you running away from something?"

"I'm not running away from anything," I said, and brushed aside his accusation by waving my hand high in front of me.

"All right, the only thing I am running away from is boredom."

"Boredom, yes," he said, grinning good-naturedly and nodding his head. "Boredom is a good thing to run away from."

We approached the rest of the party. Kurt now walked arm in arm with Else in the deeper sand. Elizabeth lagged behind them, closer to the water, drawn into herself with the cold.

"There's just one problem," Hans said.

"And what's that?"

"Sooner or later you will run right into the very thing that you are trying to escape."

He had been looking at the others then abruptly turned to me and gently touched my shoulder. "Come, let's catch up. Kurt!..." He called something to him in Danish.

Kurt and Else stopped and turned around. We reached Elizabeth first.

"Where's the bird?" I asked.

"Over there." Elizabeth pointed behind me, and we went to find the bird.

The large seagull lay on its side and must have been there for a long time. Its feathers were split and gray with dirt. Otherwise, it was relatively intact, being too cold here for any predators to have consumed it. The face, with its eye open, stared straight up at a sky that it would no longer know.

Elizabeth and I looked sadly at it in silence.

"Come," Elizabeth said, "enough of this."

She took my hand and turned me towards the water.

Kurt, Else and Hans walked together in front of us, heading back to the house.

Elizabeth slipped her arm through mine and held onto me with her other hand. This gesture felt very sweet to me, but when I turned around to meet her eyes they were red and wet, and I didn't know if this was a sudden overflow of feeling or the result of the bitter cold, stinging ocean winds. I thought it better not to ask.

At the house, Kurt unlocked the garage door. Else helped him lift it. They went inside while Hans stood at the entrance watching as Elizabeth and I walked the stone path that led to the back of the house.

Elizabeth let go of my arm. "We get the table now. Then we will go. Ah, it is so nice to have this table."

We passed Hans, as she said this. Kurt came out of the garage and said something to Hans. Hans stared at me hard, gave Elizabeth a bemused smile, then turned his back on us and followed Kurt into the garage.

The two-car garage had no room for any car, being filled to the brim with furniture and beach gear—umbrella, lounge chairs, and even a tiny sailboat. The small pine table was wedged against the back wall behind a tall bureau and two dining chairs, and Kurt and Hans struggled with it and had to lift it over the dresser. Else found the legs and the job was done. We quickly loaded table and parts into the back of the car, locked up the garage and were off again.

Everyone was quite happy to drive the two hours

back into the city and thought nothing of this extravagant caravan to transport a simple table. The conviviality did not lag amongst this party for a minute. I don't know what they found to talk about, and I would not know since they spoke a language that I would never understand. The unintelligible hum finally put me to sleep. I was tired from the ride and the long, difficult walk on the beach.

I woke up about twenty minutes before we reached the city. I noticed that Hans was asleep, slumped against the door. Else was sitting very close to Kurt, with her arm behind him on the back of the seat.

"You slept well?" Elizabeth asked.

"I guess so. How are you?"

"Very good."

"You're not tired?"

"Maybe a little. The sea air is so good for you."

I agreed but then suggested that it's a much nicer place when it's warm, and one can swim.

"You have so many rules," she said. "The ocean is always there for you—even in winter. So you can't swim, but you can still dream."

When we dropped off the table at Elizabeth's house, we all got out and exchanged hugs. Elizabeth promised to call. Hans spoke little on the way back to his place, but kissed me on the cheek when he left and said how nice it had been to meet me and maybe someday we would meet again. I was most thankful to Kurt and Else for having me as their guest and driving me to the hotel, and they were most polite in return, especially Kurt who said that I was a fine person and that he was also glad to have met me. Else gave me an affectionate squeeze and waved goodbye out the window as they departed, and I decided that she was sweet and not so bad, after all.

I was glad to be alone again, in the little temporary sanctuary of my room. I took a hot bath to dispel the chill from my bones. When I returned to my room, I dressed in my warmest sweater and pants. I stood in front of the mirror over the sink brushing my hair for a few minutes. Then I put the brush on the glass shelf, held onto the edges of the sink, and looked at my face as close as I could without going blurry-eyed. I stared at myself hard, trying to see what Hans had seen—my "look"—but try as I may I could see nothing but the same old face I always knew.

Chapter 11

I couldn't decide between the red or the deep teal. The shop girl patiently waited as I held up first one then the other sweater against my chest in front of the floor-length mirror.

"You can try them on," she said, urging me towards a decision.

I had been in the sweater shop for at least a half hour, ogling the busy and complicated hand-knit designs. They were incredibly beautiful, and I must have investigated every style, pattern, and color in the store.

The young woman had followed me like a patient lamb from every table and rack. This had only added pressure to my indecisiveness. I responded with "oh, yes," and "that's nice, too" whenever she enthusiastically showed me yet another sweater and suggested that maybe I would like *this* one. The only other customer–a middle-aged American woman–was similarly shadowed by a second saleswoman. I'm sure my lamb was very anxious for the sale. I'm also sure she had read the covetous look in my eye when I entered, for as soon as I saw them I knew that I wanted one of these luxurious sweaters. That morning I wanted everything I saw. I was in such a happy and acquisitive mood.

I had attributed this mood to the sunshine. I had slept like a rock and woken up wonderfully restored. The sea air had been good for me. I wasn't as convinced about the company. I was glad that I would never have to be with that aberrant group again, especially Hans. I couldn't say that I had enjoyed being intimidated by him. I disliked men like that, who thought that they knew everything and you, too. No wonder Else had left him. No woman would feel safe with Hans. And he was probably overbearing in bed.

A chill passed through me at the thought of making love to Hans, and I had pulled the covers over me while sitting up against the pillows.

My first hint of a sunny day was a stream of light that spilled from the edge of the drapes and caught my eye. It took me a second to register that the sun was shining, which struck me as an abnormality after all the dark days. I opened the drapes and darted back under the warm covers. The sunlight overexposed the room. I had never seen my quarters in bald daylight. It looked even worse, even more stark and lacking in warmth, and all its imperfections were only more glaring–those pimply white plaster walls, that bare tiled floor, mottled beige with liver spots. What perverse designer had imposed this vision on the world?

I rushed out into the sunshine, not pausing to eat breakfast. The sun was such a novelty, and I wanted to feel the warm rays bake my face. Of course, it was only winter sunshine, seducing me with its illusion of warmth. In fact, the air felt much colder that I had expected. Perhaps it was the penetrating cold that had made me long for the finely hand-knit woolens. I agreed to try on the sweaters.

The shop girl led me to the dressing room, and I was relieved when she left me alone there.

The spacious rooms were covered with mirrors on the three walls. On the door hung a large coat hook. Glaring overhead lights made the room unbearably bright. The encompassing mirrors left no escape from having to face every angle of my image.

I had always thought that dressing rooms were perfect torture chambers and that if ever one wanted to break a person's spirit and make them surrender all one would have to do is lock them inside a dressing room, forcing them to contemplate their multiple reflections day and night. At least in those days, I could not think of a more painful torture than this ultimate self-confrontation.

The red was a pullover with a white snowflake design. It was a very pretty wine red and fit nicely. But now that I had it on I realized how traditional and ordinary it was, and the teal—poised confidently on its hanger and boldly standing out from the hook as if a body were already in it—lured me.

The teal was a long cardigan with round half-sphere

silver buttons. From the neck down to the shoulders a fish scale design in a lighter blue and white, like a bib of chain mail, dipped into a deep sea of teal below. I had never seen anything like it before. When I put it on I felt transformed. I'm not sure why—the strange pattern, the deep color, seeing myself in something new and foreign. I felt like I was wearing a new skin. I stood there for a long time, checking front, back, side, a number of times. I don't know what I expected to see. I liked the newness of it, the strong design, and I didn't want to take it off and put the old sweater on again, whose fawn color seemed so dull in comparison and not really like me anymore.

When I handed the teal sweater to the shop girl, she beamed and ran off with it to the cash register. Over the transaction at the counter we tossed between us a profusion of thank you's like spring petals, and then I left.

I continued to shop for the rest of the morning, though I dared not spend any more. Secure in my one extravagant purchase, I now ventured into the expensive specialty shops I had previously avoided that were full of more hand-made and exquisite things—glassware, pottery, tapestries, hand-woven scarves, bowls and boxes made of teak and rosewood smooth and polished as marble and smelling of linseed oil. I admired everything, bought nothing, and left each shop feeling extremely rich. I floated up and down the Strøget, browsing in every store, stopping to have lunch in a Chinese restaurant, which I couldn't resist and which served the most dreadful food but which did not stifle my lighthearted mood. I remained buoyed by my frivolousness and extravagance, and I continued to float through the shops for the rest of the afternoon.

I opened the elevator door, which revealed Elke and The Hateful Yang, who were bundled thickly in scarves and winter jackets. Elke said "hello" brightly and even The Yang smiled as I stepped out, but it was the first time I had hit ground all day, which now felt very hard beneath my feet. They suddenly hurt, and I had an urgent need to lie down as a heavy fatigue settled on me like a cloying evening dew.

I said goodbye to them as they shut the door and went directly to my room, which was now mercifully unlit again because of the angle of the afternoon sun. I closed the drapes and took off my shoes. I left my pants, sweater, and the bag with my new purchase on the empty twin bed beside me and slid between the bedclothes in my underwear.

I immediately passed out in a benumbed sleep. The last thing I remembered was my head sinking deeply into the pillow.

I woke up to the sound of Manfred pacing the hall.

It was nighttime, and I was in the darkness now. I was disoriented at first, not remembering what day it was and if it was possibly the middle of the night–or the next day? I had a slight headache, as if I had a hangover, and felt dizzy. I lay still for a while and listened to the crunching of Manfred's shoes. He had a heavy step and the noisiest leather soles that slapped the hard vinyl floor at slow and regular intervals like the flapping of a flat tire. Crunch, *slap*, crunch, *slap*, up and down the hallway from one end to the other. What on earth was he doing? The sounds faded into the distance as he went down the hall on the opposite side. I heard one door open and shut and then a second. The two boarders had met in the hall and talked loudly as they passed my door. Was it that late?

I looked at the clock on the bedside table. It was only 5:30 p.m. I advised myself that I should turn on the light and get up, but I felt comforted by the darkness of my protective cave, and I lay there not wanting to move.

The hotel phone began to ring. Crunch, *slap*, crunch, *slap*, crunch, *slap*, crunch, *slap* came quickly down the hall. I heard "Hotel Blumendahl...ja...ja..." and a string of Danish words. The receiver clicked. There was silence for a few minutes. The phone rang again. Manfred answered with a replay of "Hotel Blumendahl", and those irritating "ja's". It began to sound like an echo–BLUMENDAHL, BLUMENdahl, Blumendahl, Blumendahl... JA, JA, Ja, ja, ja. Why hadn't they changed the name? They weren't the Blumendahls. I didn't even know their last name. My room was icy. I got out of bed, wrapped myself in a bathrobe and warmed my feet in fleece slippers. I was still reluctant to turn on the light and went to the windows. Feeling concealed by the darkness, I pulled the drapes aside and looked for *The Couple In The Window*. But, of course, they were never there when I wanted them. I stood at the window, gazing at not much. I had no view. The building next door blocked my vision, and below was only a square courtyard between the two buildings, which was empty but for a few shrubs. I continued to look left and right, hoping to catch a glimpse of something, anything but the vacuum that I found.

The metallic "click" of the key turning in the lock brought me back into the room.

"I'm in here," I shouted in time to stop Manfred from entering and finding me in the dark.

I could see his stubby fingers, which gripped the edge of the door. He quickly closed it again and his muffled voice said that I had phone messages. It was his habit to put the written messages on my pillow, which seemed unnecessary somehow.

"I am so sorry. I thought you were not here. There was no light."

"It's O.K., slide them under the door."

Two slips of white paper emerged from the thin line of light at the bottom of the door. I heard Manfred retreat down the hall again. I picked them up, sat on the edge of the bed, and reluctantly turned on the lamp. For a minute they pleased me, making me hopeful that Elizabeth had called.

They were both from Olaf, one from the morning and one in the afternoon. There were two different phone numbers.

I sighed and tossed them on the lamp table. I turned my face away from the lamp, which burned my eyes. My head ached, but now I figured it was from hunger.

I retrieved my clothes from the bed and dressed again. I shoved the bag with the teal sweater into a dresser drawer and grabbed my coat from the wardrobe. I would have dinner in a nearby café. Stuffing the phone messages in my coat pocket, I shut the light.

The café smelled of sweet meat sauces and the dusty wood floor. The faint clacking of pots and dishes could be heard through the swinging kitchen door, and I couldn't ignore the frequent heavy climactic sighing of the espresso machine from behind the far counter. The small and cheap café catered to tourists and university students. When I entered, the place was crowded, and I was lucky to find a single table tucked in a corner near the kitchen, where I managed to flag a waiter and order right away.

I waited patiently for my stew to arrive and buttered a warm roll, nibbling on it like a hungry squirrel. When the food came, I ate so furiously that I hardly tasted it. Which was also why I didn't notice the tall young black man who had left his table across the room and materialized beside mine, towering over me. He was simply "there", above me, looking down on me with a very contemptuous smirk on his very beautiful face.

"Yes?" I said, my fork poised to stab yet another cube of beef.

"You are an Ameriken," he said in an African-English accent, and curled his lip.

"And...?"

"You Amerikens, you think you can go anywhere, do anything–"

"Excuse me?"

"–start wars in the third world–"

"But I–"

"Pah! Amerikens!"

He turned on his heels and sauntered back to his friends, presumably to report on my nationality, a mixed group of Danes and another young African, all men.

"Students," I muttered, just as arrogantly.

War protesters. I had managed to keep the war far from my mind. It seemed more remote here than ever. He had poured cold water on my consciousness. How out of step we were with Europe. So far no one else had brought this up to me. But he had been so unfair. I was a war protester, too. I wasn't out of step. I was beginning to hate this face that I wore. What ever was it saying? I wanted to defend myself, to show him how wrong he was, but I didn't have the nerve and couldn't imagine how to do this without looking even more foolish. After all, this was the European system–guilty until proven innocent.

I scraped my plate clean with the last bits of bread but

somehow still felt hungry, and I ordered espresso and a piece of pastry. The student's rejection of me persisted. It hung in the air like a bad odor that wouldn't dissipate.

It was the pastry that finally made me think of Olaf. He had ordered it at lunch that day, a small chocolate torte. I was aware of the two slips of paper in my pocket pulling on me, as if they were lead sinkers instead of weightless fragile tissue. I felt around in the depths of my pocket for them. They were crumpled into each other in the corner. I pressed them flat on the table and picked the one with the afternoon phone number.

I found a phone booth by the entrance and I shut the door tightly, leaving my half-finished pastry on the table across the room. I dropped three fateful coins down the hollow gullet of the phone box.

Olaf answered.

"Olaf?"

"So nice that you called. I was thinking about you. You got my messages?"

"Yes. How are you?"

"I am fine. But I am lonely today, especially when I'm thinking of you."

"Surely you have other things to think about, other friends?" I said lightly.

"Oh yes, I have other things and other friends, but none as sweet and beautiful."

"Olaf, stop–"

"Why shouldn't I tell you that? I meant to tell you the

other day but you were in such a hurry. Why are you so shy? You have nothing to hide."

"I don't know. I just am."

"Don't be shy. It doesn't suit you. You have a strong face and such intelligent eyes. Especially don't be that way with me."

"All right, if you say so."

"So, you will meet me and Elizabeth for dinner?"

"You and Elizabeth?"

"Yes. We have decided to take you to our favorite place. You will come? Tomorrow night?"

"Tomorrow?" I muttered.

I didn't know what I thought about this invitation. I frantically searched my mind for a direction–did I want to see Olaf, did I want to see Elizabeth, did I want to see them together? It was suddenly confusing. I had managed to separate them into two different spheres, and I struggled with the concept of putting them back together again.

"If tomorrow is not good, then Wednesday?"

"Wednesday. Yes, that's fine," I said without conviction.

"Good. We will meet you at the hotel at 7:00. It's not far from the restaurant. I'll call Elizabeth. Ah, I will have sweet dreams tonight. You will be well now?"

"Yes, I'll be very well."

"Then I will see you on Wednesday."

"Yes, Wednesday."

I held onto the receiver for a while after he hung up, letting the dial tone bore into my ear. Then that felt odd and I placed it back in the holder, but I didn't want to leave the phone booth. I wanted to hide there; outside felt exposing and every step now would lead me one step closer to Wednesday.

On my way back from the phone booth I couldn't avoid passing the table with the students, who were now quietly eating. I tried to ignore them and kept my face forward but was self-conscious of them stealing a glance at me.

I eyed my abandoned cake and decided to finish it off. The tiny cup of coffee was cold and I ordered another, causing the espresso machine once more to exhale a heavy sigh.

Why had I called him, and why had I said "yes" I asked myself? What was I thinking? No, I wasn't thinking. I was swimming in turbulent waters, every once in a while surfacing for air, then plunging down again to swim in yet another direction.

Olaf. Well, he wasn't Hans or even Kurt, and he was something substantial to hold onto.

The night air was a shock after the steamy restaurant. It had rained briefly but hard as I ate, and now the asphalt glistened a shiny black, mirroring the light from the street lamps and the colored neon signs. I could smell the dampness. Cars whooshed by on the wet road. I walked alone on the desolate sidewalk and watched the flickering kaleidoscopic shapes of the colored lights on the street dance by my path.

A drunken man zigzagging on the sidewalk came towards me. He was drinking from a small bottle and singing or attempting to sing. He didn't notice me, lost in the song. It was a slow, plaintive song, drawn out by his slowing mind, a sad song that seemed endless. I could still hear it for a good while after he passed me. And I missed it when I turned a corner and could hear it no longer.

Chapter 12

Tuesday passed much too quickly. I'm not sure why since I did so little–a visit to the Rosenborg Castle and the art museum across the street, all of which lasted a total of two hours. Sometimes doing nothing takes more time than plowing through a crowded day. It is strange how human beings can adjust their rhythms to the current of any new stream of life. I was able to take more time doing less with great ease.

For example, dressing now required a series of executive decisions made over long negotiations in front of the wardrobe mirror. Before that process could even begin washing and grooming were performed slowly, meticulously, and thoroughly enough to pass any country's military inspection. A simple breakfast of buttered rolls and coffee took the time of a full-course dinner.

I was in no hurry. I had lost any normal sense of time due to the vacation's open-ended schedule. There was no time. My life had stopped and time had stopped. I had stepped out of time and into a dream, a dream from which I couldn't awaken.

It was nearly 11:00 a.m. before I arrived at the castle. It was a city castle and not a fortress like Elsinore. I saw a series of obscenely garish, overly decorated living quarters and ended up standing in a small room that contained the displays of the royal treasures—gold and gem-studded bric-a-brac and the crown jewels. I had never understood the fascination with crowns and gems and could not fathom living with these things.

The thick gold sculpted crowns were so encrusted with rubies and emeralds that they must have weighed a few pounds each. I tried to imagine how it might feel to wear that much metal on my head. The closest I could come was the image of wearing a metal pot, which seemed more absurd the more I thought about it. And the jewels, they could only drag you down, those big shimmering stones. Then there was the china plate with gold leaf and the silver with the family crest and so on. After a while I began to feel wretched looking at the belongings of these dead people. There is something depressing about the fact that the owners' flesh and bones had long since disintegrated and what was left were the soulless objects of their lives. And even the objects were dead, trapped behind the glass untouched and unused.

I needed to find my way out of this tomb.

I left that room and found the throne room, a large hall with a raised platform and carved chair that was the throne and commanded all the attention. This made sense, but again I couldn't imagine what it would have felt to sit there, all powerful, commanding, absolute ruler. Did I want to sit there? No, I didn't need that. I would have been content to rule my own life, which still felt controlled by outside forces beyond my reach.

I was glad to leave the cloying atmosphere of the castle and cross the street to the modern building that was the art museum, full of windows and light and airy galleries. I was relieved to be in the 20th century again with modern paintings, abstract shapes that let you breathe and bright colors that made you feel alive.

The Munch paintings startled me though. I had never seen the originals. The colors were infinitely more shocking than in reproductions—those gaunt yellow faces and fierce red skies, acid greens and blues. They moved me to want to cry out like the criers in the paintings, and they forced me to leave.

I couldn't get the screaming yellow faces out of my mind. I wanted to scream, too. Everything around me was so quiet and peaceful, and I didn't fit in here. But then I wasn't sure I quite fit in anywhere.

By the time I got back to the hotel I was already dreading dinner. I could see that an evening with Olaf and Elizabeth would be difficult. I would have much preferred Elizabeth alone and Olaf not at all. But now it was too late for that. I had sealed my fate, and I could not turn back. Elizabeth with Olaf was better than no Elizabeth.

On my way to my room I poked my head in the lounge

to see if I could relax and read for a while. Unfortunately, Elke and Margarethe were there, sitting close together on the loveseat. At first they were so absorbed in each other that they didn't see me. As Elke spoke, Margarethe nodded her head and smiled. She was almost pretty when she smiled with those small dark eyes and full, dark eyebrows. Then Margarethe caught my eye and Elke turned around to see what she was staring at. Elke said "hi" and asked me to join them, but I declined excusing myself to my room and a nap.

"Maybe later," Elke suggested.

"Maybe."

Now that I had told this white lie I realized that I could use a nap.

I took off my clothes. My hands and feet were very cold. I rubbed my feet inside the sheets and buried them in the folds of the blankets. My hands ended up between my legs where it was naturally warm, and then got warmer.

I waited for Elizabeth and Olaf downstairs on the street. There was no need for them to come up for me, and I didn't want them to see the hotel. It was bad enough they knew where it was, on the fringes of the red light district. I hadn't known this at first but it had been pointed out to me when I got lost one day and a man whom I asked for directions back to the hotel had chuckled and explained why. How was I to know? There were no red lights here or any other indication of this. Sex shops and sexual activity knew no boundaries in this city. I was again reassured that I was safe though, here or anywhere in the city, and, besides, he added, "the women don't want you".

They were late. I wasn't surprised; Elizabeth wasn't the punctual type. I didn't mind. It was nice to have a few more moments to myself. I thought about what I would do after Copenhagen. Actually, I hadn't a clue. I was booked until Sunday and was scheduled to check out Monday morning and still hadn't decided what country to go to next. This was my great freedom plan, but the truth was that now I simply felt lost. I wasn't even sure how I would fill up the next four days. I was thankful to have a real plan for Friday night–the ballet. I had hoped to spend some time with Elizabeth, who would be available since she wasn't working, but she was so elusive and mercurial. I was surprised that she had even suggested this dinner. I would try and pin her down this time. I had yet to see her without third parties.

I saw them before they saw me. Walking arm in arm, they looked like a married couple, familiar and naturally comfortable with each other. And it still seemed a shame to me somehow that they weren't. They were so close.

Olaf waved when he saw me and let go of Elizabeth's arm. I waved at them and felt my stomach churn. I now looked forward to being at the restaurant and working on my second or third drink.

Elizabeth threw her arms around me and gave me a warm, hard squeeze. Olaf held me by the waist and kissed me lightly on the lips. Then they both grabbed an arm and led me away amidst a peppering of assurances that we were each "fine" and how good it was to see one other. Olaf squeezed my arm with his free hand and gave me a meaningful look.

"You-will-like-this-place," Elizabeth said. "It-is-the-best. Very special food–Italian. We love it. Yes, Olaf?"

"Yes."

"Whenever I am sad Olaf takes me here, and I am always better."

"It's just the wine," Olaf said and laughed.

"Don't listen to him. He is always saying things like this."

She gave him a menacing look, at which he faked a pout and turned his face forward.

"It's not far," he said, "only a few more blocks and then to the left."

Elizabeth and Olaf carried me along. I swore my feet weren't touching the ground, and I was propelled by a strong wind. They were both determined to entertain me, Olaf with a story about winning a big account that day at the studio and Elizabeth saying how much fun it had been to have me on Sunday and that she was enjoying her new table. Dividing my attention between them confounded me, as I didn't know to whom I owed my allegiance or how to remain independent of both of them.

Elizabeth smelled of a sweet, floral perfume that swept over me when the wind blew in my direction. I would lean near her every once in a while to breath it again. The scent blended well with her skin and gave the effect of being the odor of her body. I wanted to bury my face in her neck as I would have in a bouquet of fragrant flowers.

I liked the restaurant. The waiters were friendly and the atmosphere was dark. A bottle of red wine arrived as soon as we sat down and were handed menus. Without asking, Olaf filled our glasses, which we each spontaneously clinked together.

"To wonderful friends," Elizabeth said and drank a liberal portion of her glass.

"To wonderful friends," I responded holding my glass towards both of them.

I followed Elizabeth's lead and drank my first glass rather quickly. The dry red wine went down easily. As I had hoped, my second glass planted me in the seat. Olaf sat beside me, and I was face to face with Elizabeth, whose eyes seemed even a deeper blue than I remembered and larger than life.

We all ordered different kinds of pasta, and I was happy when bread arrived but surprised to see a second bottle replace the empty first one so soon. These two drank wine like soda, and I would never keep up with them.

I was starving and the wine made me hungrier and decidedly dreamier. I soon fell into that half-conscious state between knowing and not knowing where I was. The world already seemed like I was viewing it through thick uneven glass.

"You look very nice tonight," Olaf said.

"Of course she does," Elizabeth added. "She is always so pretty."

"And you both look pretty, too," I said, to which they laughed.

"You are such a hard girl," Olaf said. "And much too modest. I can't tell you anything. It all bounces off."

I shrugged my shoulders and took another sip of wine.

"So, my friend," Elizabeth said, "are you enjoying the city?"

I assured her that I was and then went into a detailed description of the past few days as the food arrived.

Elizabeth "mmmed" when her plate of spaghetti and meatballs was positioned under her chin but left it waiting while she consumed yet another half glass of wine.

Olaf had no trouble simultaneously imbibing wine and eating and managing to watch my progress too, encouraging me with more bread and making sure that I was happy with everything.

I was faced with a mountain of fettuccine, which would have lasted me easily for two dinners, and a very dainty salad of a few greens and scattered bits of tomato and onions. But my appetite had waned. I dabbed at my pasta and only a stray fork landed in the salad bowl every now and then.

"Eat, eat. You don't like the food?" Olaf said, filling my glass to the brim before it was drained by a half.

"Oh no, it's delicious. It's just too much."

"Never too much food. You can never have too much food or too much love."

He winked at me and reached for a slab of Italian bread.

Elizabeth finally began to stir the spaghetti and eat a meatball. I watched for signs of an ensuing drunkenness on her part, but she appeared to be amazingly stable that night. I was the one whose mind was slowly dissolving from the alcohol. I ate more food, hoping to regain some consciousness, but I had an increasingly hard time feeling altogether whole.

The waiter stopped at our table with an empty drink tray in one hand. Olaf asked for something, which, as I suspected, turned out to be a third bottle of wine.

The place filled up now with other diners, people who could have been the brothers and sisters of Olaf and Elizabeth, though blonder and older. The bare wood floors created a hollow din, which, with my dulling senses, sounded like a thousand voices echoing from the deep, not unlike the sound of a seashell held to the ear. I lost myself in the noise and concentrated on the smooth cream sauce and soft noodles that warmed my mouth, eased down my throat, and sated me.

Olaf replenished our glasses from the new bottle, but I had reached my capacity and ignored mine. Olaf pushed his empty plate away from him and planted his wine glass in its place.

"You-are-so-quiet," Elizabeth said to me. "You are thinking, I know. I myself also think too much. Too-much-thinking-is-bad."

"Bad?"

"Yes, it-is-bad-for-the-ah, ah, English. I don't know how to say it in English. Olaf, how do you say....." She said a Danish word.

"Cir-cu-la-tion," he said to her carefully, as if he were instructing a beloved student.

"Yes, bad for the cir-cu-la-tion," which she pronounced slowly to make her point. "When you are thinking all the time, too much blood gets caught in your brain."

She put her hands on both temples for emphasis.

"Then your brain is stuck and your head gets very heavy and you think you are only this brain and your whole life is in this little brain. Your arms and your legs they don't move and now you can't even think anymore because there is so much blood stuck in your mind. Oh, yes, thinking is very bad. I make little thinking. What good is all this thinking anyway? It tells you nothing."

At first I thought this was a joke, but she had said it with a straight face.

Olaf looked at her thoughtfully and stroked his beard.

"So what do you do when you're not thinking, now that you're not thinking so much?" I asked.

"I do what I have to do. If I am writing, I write. If I

am sitting, I sit. If I am walking, I walk. If I am talking to you, I talk to you. I live, that is what I do. That is all you have to do. And not thinking about living. If you are thinking about living you are not living. Ah, I am so bad in English. I cannot say this good in English."

"You said it fine," I assured her, though I could see how she was struggling with her ideas and they were not all passing through the language barrier, like refugees escaping over the Berlin wall: some were making it and some were caught on the other side. I longed to know more of Elizabeth's mind, which, like she said, was weak in English and clearly so strong and wise in her own language. I felt shut out of a country I would never know.

"When are you leaving?" Olaf asked, raising the bottle toward my glass again.

"No, really–I can't drink anymore."

"Come, come, it's only a little wine."

He gently brushed my hand away from the glass and filled it to the top. I attempted a few sips but really had more than enough. I could feel the dizziness coming on and reached for more food to save me again from sinking too far.

"And when are you leaving?" he asked again.

"Monday," I said between bites. "Monday morning. That's when I'm supposed to check out".

"So soon? Where are you going?"

"I don't know. I haven't made up my mind yet."

I had put down my fork. I couldn't eat another bite. In

fact I had eaten too much food and the rich cream sauce sat like a sunken lump in my stomach.

"You are such a brave girl," Elizabeth said. "You go and there you are and you don't know anyone. I could never do this."

"No, I'm not brave. I'm indecisive. I can't decide what I want to do next."

"So stay here," Olaf suggested. "One more week?"

"I can't. I don't have time, and there's so much I want to see—London, Amsterdam, Paris...I really can't."

"Ah, Paris. Yes, you must see Paris."

Elizabeth pointed her wineglass at me then held it in front of her face, eyeing it before she drank again.

"Paris is so beautiful," she said.

"Paris is very beautiful, but Copenhagen has much better people," Olaf insisted, turning to face me.

"Very-good-people," Elizabeth said, nodding.

I had to agree.

Elizabeth and I finally pushed our plates away and Olaf asked for the bill, which he paid after a liberal protest from us. Standing outside the restaurant, he offered to take us to a café for coffee and dessert and without thinking I said that sounded fine.

"Oh, no, Olaf," Elizabeth said, surprisingly. "It is too late for me. I am so tired now."

"It's not that late. Just come for a little while. Don't leave yet."

I put my hand on her shoulder as if that would

somehow change her mind.

But she insisted again that we would linger, it would get late, and she had to get up early.

Olaf hailed a cab for her and handed the driver a bill. Then he hugged her and opened the car door.

I leaned in to say goodbye to her and she hugged me and begged me to call her the next day. I swore that I would as she kissed my cheek. I drank in another whiff of her sweet scent before the door slammed and the car stole her away.

Elizabeth stuck her head out the window and waved, and we both waved back.

I suddenly felt awkward standing alone on the busy street with Olaf. People passed us by on both sides, and I already missed Elizabeth.

"I have another idea," Olaf said, grabbing my shoulders.

"What?"

"Let's have the coffee at my place."

"Your place?"

Olaf held onto my shoulders. I wondered if he was going to let go. He smiled down at me with a look that could only be described as innocent desire, if there was such a thing.

"I don't know, Olaf. I'm not feeling too well–the wine..."

I put my hand to my forehead to show him exactly where I was not well. The food had not kept me from

sinking. My mind was now fathoms below its normal
surface of consciousness and at that depth was navigating
very slowly on a course that was dark and murky, from
which I couldn't find the way out.

He released my shoulders and gently plucked my hand
from my forehead and then caressed my cheek.

"The coffee will make you feel better."

He continued to smooth my cheek, to stroke my hair,
letting his hand fall on my shoulder, then down the length
of my arm, catching my fingers.

I could feel the warmth of his hand through my glove.
His grip was strong but tender. In spite of my resistance,
this was comforting. I felt myself sinking deeper into a
fog, and I needed something firm to hold onto.

"Yes?" he said.

"All right, just for a little while."

"Good."

He squeezed my hand and we walked to the corner,
where he managed to stop a cab right away. Before I knew
it I was heading to the other side of the city, to Olaf's
comfortable and masculine apartment. I might as well
have been traveling to the other side of the universe, for
all I knew, my mind was so muddy. I closed my eyes and
rested my head on the back of the seat.

"Don't go to sleep yet," he whispered in my ear.

I opened my eyes and looked at him. His face was
feverish from all the wine, but on Olaf this looked healthy.

"I'm not sleeping. I'm dizzy."

"I will fix that."

He took my head and placed it on his chest, rubbing my temples, and held me in that position for the rest of the ride.

He was right—it took away my dizziness—but now I did want to sleep, to fade into that sweet submerged nothingness from which I always safely returned. Olaf was quiet as he rubbed my head but asked every once in a while if I was sleeping, to which I replied no, as I struggled not to succumb to that peaceful oblivion.

I found myself in familiar surroundings, but it was an uncomfortable familiarity that said "I've been here before and I'm not sure I want to be here again."

Olaf left me alone in the living room while he went to make coffee. Sitting on the sofa, I felt a sense of dread and foreboding, an overwhelming feeling that it was wrong of me to come, and this alarming feeling woke me up even before Olaf reappeared cheerfully with two white china cups and saucers, which he gingerly placed on the table in front of me.

"Drink now; you'll feel better."

I drank but I knew I would not feel any better, especially since I knew that he only wanted me to feel better so that he could make me feel even better.

"Very good coffee," I noted.

"Yes, well, Danish coffee is some of the best."

"Yes, I know. I like it."

He watched me pensively while I drank the coffee and didn't take his eyes off me as I returned the cup to its saucer.

"Do you like me?" he asked.

"What do you mean?" I asked defensively, as if this were some kind of accusation.

"I mean—do you like me?"

"Of course I like you. Why would I be with you if I didn't like you?"

Olaf shrugged.

"There could be a lot of reasons. I am not sure you like me. Sometimes you are warm and sometimes you are somewhere else. You are a very hard girl to know. But maybe that is why I like you. You are not a simple girl."

"I'm sorry, I don't mean to be like that."

I truly felt badly that he could sense my moments of retreat.

"It's all right. But don't be that way now. Is your head better?" he asked, stroking the top of my head gently.

"Yes, it's much better," I said, trying to ignore his touch, which had sent ripples down the back of my neck.

He kissed my forehead, my nose, my cheeks, then my lips, where he stayed for a long while...

I didn't resist. Kissing Olaf was easier than talking to him at that moment. I liked Olaf's kisses. He had instinctively the right touch in whatever he did. I kissed

149

him back and found myself sinking again. This time I was pressed under by the rock of Olaf's desire, a rock I wanted to cling to and jump off at the same time. But which? Which? And why did I feel this way? Olaf's warm hands on my skin only conflicted me further, soft and slow moving, soothing sensitive hands caressing my back, unhooking my bra, circling my breasts...I was sinking, sinking, sinking, into the waves, waves of feeling spewing from my depths and washing over the front of my body, sinking under the weight of the feelings... I gave into the waves. I lay back on the sofa and Olaf came over me, pushed my sweater up and kissed me everywhere, covering my skin with little warm wet kisses. He made low groaning noises and continued to undress me, unzipping my pants and nuzzling his face on my belly. I lay there with my eyes closed, was lost in that dark world of sexual feeling, Olaf swimming on top of me, with his whole body. I was sinking again then thought, no, I should be swimming, swimming with Olaf, we should be swimming together like two playful porpoises. Instead I was sinking, going under, under, clinging to a rock...

My last thought before the storm was: nothing grows on a rock and it has no heartbeat.

Olaf sat up for a minute to tear off his sweater and his shirt while my eyes were closed, and I didn't expect him to press his body so firmly against mine, kissing me and holding me close. The cushions moved under me and I suddenly felt like I was in the hold of a boat in a hurricane, and I do poorly on water in good weather. The waves became waves of nausea–the wine, the food. They swept me off the rock.

I pushed Olaf aside, pulled down my sweater and ran to the bathroom holding my mouth with my hand and just making it to the toilet where I vomited the contents of my guts, wretched and wretched again, until there was nothing left to wretch but my soul.

Olaf found me clutching the rim of the toilet bowl after having disposed of my insides.

"Are you O.K.?" he asked, alarmed.

"I'm all right. I drank too much."

"Let me help you."

He picked me up. I rinsed the vile taste out of my mouth with tap water and Olaf walked me back to the sofa.

"Come, I have some tea for this."

"No, please. I just want to sit still."

"You must let me do something for you. You are ill. Here, sit."

He left me on the sofa, went to the bathroom and returned with a wet washcloth and sat down next to me.

"Put your head here," he said, patting his lap.

I was too weak to argue with him. I lay on my back with my head in Olaf's lap and he placed the soothing, cool cloth on my forehead.

"That feels nice."

"I am so sorry you are not well."

"I am, too. I've ruined your evening."

"No, you could never ruin my evening."

"You don't know," I said, looking up at him, the back of my fingers grazing his cheek, his simple peasant's beard.

"You really don't know."

Olaf persisted in trying to get me to spend the night, but I adamantly refused insisting that it would be best if I went back to the hotel. He finally let me go and called a cab for me, begging me to please call him in the morning to let him know how I was.

"Thank you for everything. And don't worry about me, I'm fine."

"Yes, you are fine," he said, hugging me tightly against his chest. "You are very fine."

I was anything but fine. I was dizzy and still horribly seasick. My head was a block of cast iron that someone pounded against with a hammer. I dreaded how I would feel in the morning. I was grateful that it was still early enough for me to get a full night's sleep.

I was glad to be back in my private, cold little cell. I turned on the garish lamp next to the bed. The drapes were open for some reason and when I went to close them there they were—*The Couple in the Window*—as usual, when I least expected them. And then they did a very strange thing. They were both seated, reading newspapers. First he then she put their papers down. They stood up and faced each other. Then they both walked to the window and, each taking an end of the cloth, walked towards each other and closed the curtains. Then the light went out.

I knew, with a knowing that came from my whole being, that I would never see them again and that I would never be like them.

Never.

Chapter 13

The room was spinning. I gripped the bedclothes and closed my eyes to stop the motion, but as soon as I opened them I was once more on a carousel that was speeding out of control. I thought I would be sick again, and this time I wouldn't make it to the bathroom down the hall.

There were two tap-taps on the door followed by Elke's voice.

"Hello? Are you there?"

"Yes," I shouted.

"I will come again later."

I could hear the clacking of her pumps fade away. Elke was the only woman I knew who did housework in pumps.

Was it that late already that Elke would be changing beds? I managed to turn my head towards the clock. Yes, it was that late.

I felt like I was wearing one of those leaden royal crowns, which was now stuck to the top of my head, never to come off. There was a metallic ringing in my ears.

Another knock. This one more deliberate and louder.

"Yes?"

"Can you come to telephone? Someone is calling," Manfred bellowed through the door.

"No, I can't. Will you please take a message?"

I could hear him convey my response in Danish.

Another knock. Would they never end?

"He says call this morning. Here is the number."

He slid the note under the door.

"Thank you."

Opening one eye I contemplated the tiny white flag but made no attempt to get up. I clung to the faith that inertia would cure me. I knew I would have to move eventually, if only to go to the bathroom, and I dreaded the thought. I lay in bed and tried to keep my eyes open.

I felt extremely tired and weary. The more I thought about the night before, the more it seemed like a dream and the worst sort of dream it became, the kind of bad dream that puts you in a foul mood immediately on awakening. I wanted it to slip from my memory. I wished it to be one of those dreams that escape you on waking even though you know you have dreamed something, even something significant, but something that has shown its face only to recede into the depths of the unconscious, from which it may surface again or remain forever buried.

However, the vision of that night arose in me unmercifully vivid. I wanted to turn away from it and happily anticipated leaving it thousands of miles behind.

I peered again at the piece of paper by the door, waving its acid white tongue at me, vying for my attention.

What on earth made me do these things? Why was I such a vacillating little fish, swimming alternately this way and that through the waters of life, waters that were so calm and clear before I entered them?

I needed some juice or coffee or both and I would have to go out for them. Obviously, I had missed breakfast. I lay in bed long enough to attempt some movement. Then, cautiously, gingerly, I raised myself, put my legs over the side of the bed, and stood up. My head still clanged, but I was off the carousel and finally capable of forward motion. I wrapped my robe tightly around me and was about to open the door when I stopped and spied Olaf's message on the floor by my feet. For a second I hesitated, then snatched it up, crushed it in my hand and threw it in the wastebasket under the sink.

That day and the next I managed to do an awful lot of nothing. I secluded myself in steamy cafes, read the wolf book while drinking carafes of coffee and definitely ate too much pastry. To be truthful, I had slept most of Thursday. I continued to feel ill most of that day, and my headache persisted well into the evening.

I could not reach Elizabeth by phone Thursday or all

morning Friday. By Friday afternoon I grew so frustrated by this that I decided to risk a call later that night, after I returned from the ballet. So like Elizabeth to ask me to call and then disappear. I wondered how one carried on any kind of friendship with her, she always being an arm's length away. I had to admit that the thought of attending the ballet excited me–something real to do. Now I was glad I had packed the dress and heels that everyone else insisted I would need and that I only included out of feeling obliged to follow this well-meaning advice.

I decided to go "all out" for the occasion, as if this were somehow a romantic date with a special lover, instead of an evening out by myself. I even went to the trouble of buying special shampoo and lavender-scented bath beads in the shape of fat violet pearls at a chic toiletry shop that I had passed on my meanderings that morning.

These preparations began in the late afternoon since my long, thick hair would take hours to dry. I luxuriated in the bathtub with bubbles up to my nose as I inhaled the lavender perfume that smelled good enough to drink.

I finally felt completely free of any deleterious effects of that night of excess, and the foamy, sweet bath had restored my good mood. It was as if I had been drinking the bubbles. I only reluctantly washed my hair and drained the tub. But the shampoo, too, was wonderfully scented and I left the bathroom feeling clean and fragrant. I was sure that I emitted a jet stream of perfumed air behind me as I traveled down the hallway.

Back in the room, I sat on the bed and towel-dried my hair. Warmed from the hot bath, I untied my robe and threw it with the towel on the chair by the night stand. I fluffed up the pillows and sat back against them, stretching my legs out. I relished being naked and free again. I hadn't seen my body in weeks; the room was usually too cold to be undressed.

What a surprise to suddenly see my flesh—so familiar and so strange to me at once. I thought of being with Olaf the other night, and the first time, his touching me, making love...but it didn't feel like anything that had happened to my body, as if all that had only happened in my mind. My body didn't remember it.

I could smell the lavender on my skin, an almost imperceptible light smell. I loved how warm I felt, and I didn't want my body to cool down, which it would do, especially since I had exposed it to the cool air. I covered myself with the sheet and blankets in an attempt to capture the warmth for as long as it would last. I held the back of my hand to my nose to smell the lavender again. It vaguely reminded me of Elizabeth's alluring perfume. Perhaps I would ask her what it was and take some home with me.

The relaxing bath and my body heat under the warm covers lulled me to sleep. I fell deeply into a dream. I believed in this dream...

I am really here. I am walking on a frozen beach but it is warm and sunny. The beach is frozen because the waves have rolled

onto the sand and have become ice, frozen in motion. They are big
ice sculptures of spumy, rolling waves. They are in my path and I
have to walk around them, climb over them. I am naked but I don't
mind; the sun feels good on my skin. I see two people walk towards
me. As they get closer, I recognize the Blumendahls. They are fully
dressed in street clothes. I am afraid they will see me, I need to hide.
I suddenly feel ashamed to be naked and exposed like this. There is
a forest next to the beach. I gauge whether I can run into the forest
quickly enough before they see me. They keep walking towards me,
arm in arm, smiling. I make a mad dash for the woods and crouch
low behind a tree. I cover myself with my long hair to hide and
protect me. But... it's not a tree: it's Olaf! He kisses me. I kiss him
back, then stop. I apologize and say that I like him very much but I
have to leave now. I feel guilty about this. Then he disappears...

I woke up. It was time to dress.

First I had to trim my toenails, then file my fingernails.
Then I had to arrange my clothes on the bed and place my
black heels on the floor standing up. I dug into my jewelry
bag for the plain gold chain and the gold hoop earrings,
which I laid delicately on the dress to see what I thought.
I approved.

My hair was still slightly damp so I fluffed it up to let
more air through the wet curly mass. I decided to wear some
makeup, which I rarely did, favoring the natural look of
the times—a dash of eyeliner, rose pink-colored powdered
blush, and a darker rose lipstick. I covered myself with all
the smaller items, and then the dress. It was a black knit

that wrapped sleekly around me and tied in front, crossed tightly over the bodice, which gave it a low v-neck, clinging to me snug as a leotard. I usually didn't buy such revealing clothing, but I had been in a dating phase at the time. I only chose to bring it on the trip because it was simple and the knit didn't wrinkle. After weeks of submerging my body in sweaters and a heavy coat, it was charming to have a shape again. And even I couldn't help but notice that the dress had a flattering fit.

Then there was my hair–long and wavy and parted down the middle--which was wrong somehow and too casual for my outfit. I couldn't think of a way to make it more elegant. I was never good at creating "up" styles, and if I tried they usually fell down in the middle of the evening. The most I could manage was to obliterate the part, comb the top and sides back into a long tail, which I clipped with a flat plastic tortoise shell barrette, with the remainder falling behind my shoulders and halfway down my back, waving behind me like a long, dark banner of my femininity.

I deliberately chose a three-star restaurant near the theatre, which "the book" had recommended for its excellence but warned against for its higher prices. Well, I had a discount ballet ticket, I argued with my tourist budget self.

It was one of those establishments that was hushed by an abundance of carpeting and drapery in somber reds and deep blues and forested in greenery that spilled over huge ceramic urns and small trees that posed formally in dark corners. Round tables wore long white linens like formal gowns and were crowned with tall candles and bunches of fresh flowers in miniature milk glass vases.

I was led to a small table set for two, where a waiter stood behind me as I sat down and then pushed in my chair. A chorus of waiters, who wore short white jackets and close fitting black pants attended to me. They were all very handsome and moved with choreographed gestures and never seemed to sweat no matter how many times they spun through the padded kitchen doors and back carrying enormous round trays heavily laden with a whole table's worth of dinners.

I thoroughly delighted in the pampering and extravagance to which I had rewarded myself. After a scrumptious meal, I left feeling that I had indeed made a very queenly and wise choice and that it had been the perfect way to start a perfect evening.

The theatre was packed. It was a while before I arrived at my seat in one of the upper galleries. I had never been in such an enormous hall. Balconies and galleries rose row after row like an endless wedding cake. My seat was located at a dizzying height. The stage below appeared too tiny to hold a troupe of dancers. I wondered whether I'd be able to see anything at all, when the lights suddenly went down. The curtain rose, the music started, and a gang of pirates danced onto the stage.

It was a men's dance, very energetic with difficult gestures and sword fights. The dance fascinated me and completely absorbed my attention.

One exquisite dance followed another. It was all too stirring and beautiful—beautiful movements, beautiful men, beautiful women, in beautiful multicolored costumes, spun, floated, flew across the stage. When the house lights came up for intermission, I found myself on the edge of my seat, clinging to the banister of the row in front of me.

I should have gotten up and stretched my legs with the hordes of people around me who had popped out of their seats and milled about the theatre, stood in bathroom lines and bought drinks at the small bar. But I couldn't move. I was afraid of losing the beauty that had drifted up to my heavenly seat like a cool, sweet ocean breeze and gave just the right touch of relief from a strong, dry heat. I felt light and angelic and I didn't want to feel the hard ground.

The second half of the program was equally as exciting as the first—large numbers with lots of lifting, leaping movements across the stage. The last dance captivated me the most. Two dancers, a man and a woman, acted like butterflies in a mating dance. They weren't dressed like butterflies but they moved like them, with light, fluid movements. They were together—apart—together—apart— and together again as he finally "caught" her, and they danced under and over their bodies and slowly, tenderly folded into each other.

I was feeling warm and unconsciously breathing deeply. An emotional lump formed in my throat, and I began to cry.

I had never experienced anything so beautiful or so romantic, everything–the poignant strings, the dancers, the motions–all woven together with fine, delicate threads like an intricate lace pattern.

Then it was over. Lights up, curtain down. Curtain calls. The audience sprang to its feet for an extended standing ovation. I stood with the rest and clapped so hard that my hands stung afterward.

I descended the winding staircase from the gallery but its height stayed with me, and the lofty feelings of the dances. Everything had been so beautiful and moving, pushed to the edges of pleasure that bordered on pain. The people around me had also been beautiful with their pretty clothes, their perfume and cologne that permeated the atmosphere, their tall blond elegance. My feet did not feel the carpeted stairs. I wanted to dance, too. I wanted to float back to the hotel on my toes. But I walked in the usual manner: feet flat on the ground.

I couldn't wait to call Elizabeth and tell her about my evening, and I couldn't stop smiling. Everyone I passed on the street said "hello" to me and I said "hello" back, in a friendly manner.

When I opened the glass door to the hotel, the harsh overhead lighting startled me, and I blinked hard.

"Hello," Elke shouted and waved from the lounge.

She was at the table across from Manfred. They were drinking beer from green, stubby bottles. Elke drank hers from a glass, as usual.

"Come, join us," Elke beckoned me again.

"On the house," Manfred said, lifting his beer bottle.

"On the house" appealed to me after such an extravagant evening. In my elevated mood, I even had a loving eye that night for Elke and Manfred, the happy couple, she so pretty and he so compliant. And look how generous they were; they did mean well, after all.

Elke smiled ardently at me, then at Manfred.

I reached inside the small refrigerator, which was stocked with beer and soft drinks, took one bottle of beer and opened it with the church-key that hung on the refrigerator door. I chose to sit at the head of the table, Manfred to my left and Elke to my right. My two neighbors, the middle-aged boarders, sat on the loveseat and also drank beer in front of the glaring and very loud TV.

"To your hospitality," I toasted them, drinking from the bottle like Manfred.

They toasted me back.

"Such a pretty dress," Elke said, leaning back to get a fuller look at me.

"Thank you," I said, smiling at Elke.

"This dress is very good on you. Don't you think so, Manfred?"

"Very pretty," Manfred said, glancing in my direction.

"Thank you," I said again, giving him a warm smile, too.

I swigged another large mouthful of beer. It was the kind I had been drinking that afternoon in the pub—very tasty and very strong.

"So, you have been out?" Elke said as she emptied the bottle into her glass.

"Yes, I have–to the ballet."

"Aah, how good. And you went with a man?"

"Oh, no. I went by myself."

"By yourself?" She squeezed her eyebrows into a deep, astonished frown. "Manfred, did you hear that? She went to the ballet by herself."

Manfred sat stony-faced as a sphinx and stared into space, his fat paws fisted on the table except when he occasionally raised the green bottle to his lips.

He "hmmmed" and nodded at her.

Elke finished her glass of beer, too quickly I thought. Manfred immediately rose, carried the empty bottle away and returned with a fresh one for Elke and another for me. I also hurriedly finished the remainder of my bottle. The walking had made me thirsty and I wanted to be equal to Elke, although it was beginning to dawn on me that she already had had more than the one that had just been replaced. She had spoken slower than usual and she would alternately lean slightly left then right, unable to straighten herself totally upright.

I resented Elke's prying questions and accusations about not having an escort for the ballet, which had caused in me an uncomfortably descending mood. Gravity struck, and I lost the ability to fly. Watching Elke sway like a ship in a restless sea also created a less than uplifting sensation.

She had soiled the purity of my mood, and I regretted having sat down with them.

I drank liberally from my bottle, which created the now desired effect of my feeling less and less of anything by the moment.

"It doesn't matter. I still had a lovely evening."

"Of course you did," Elke insisted.

The boarders talked loudly to each other, in spite of the chattering TV, and I was glad that they were too distracted and too distant to overhear our conversation. The heat began to rise through the pipes, which caused them to knock loudly every few minutes, like gongs announcing some momentous event.

Manfred's eyes strayed to the TV set, while Elke and I worked diligently at our beers. When we finished our bottles, they were again amiably replaced by Manfred, who accepted this subservient role. I had yet to understand Manfred, his ponderous passivity, his self-contained reticence, his large, dull eyes that were ever aware of my presence and that said nothing.

I had deflated down to sea level with Elke. I didn't care. My beautiful evening was over.

Elke gave me an inebriated grin. Then she closed her eyes and drank. The way she lifted her arm and tilted her head made me think of the dancers. She was as thin as they were and her movement as fluid, though hers was the result of drunkenness, not of practiced grace. Even so, there was still something delicate and lovely about Elke, something angelic and otherworldly, certainly a world that I didn't know.

"Why don't you want a man?" she asked me, suddenly opening her eyes.

"Who said that? They don't want me," I blurted before I knew what I was saying. I didn't even know I thought this.

"I don't believe this. You are so pretty," she said, whispering the word "pretty".

Manfred studied Elke's face but didn't say anything. She seemed not to notice and kept her gaze on me.

Elke's dark pupils had become large murky ponds that almost obliterated her pale aqua-blue irises. She had moved her chair to the edge of the table and leaned close to me.

I shrugged.

"Not really."

"Oh, yes, really. Manfred says—"

"Elke." Manfred shot a warning glance in her direction. "Another?"

He retrieved my empty bottle from the table before I could answer.

I didn't care. I had lost track of the how-many's, and was sinking again, sinking into Elke's ponds.

Elke scrutinized my face. I concentrated on my hands, with which I unconsciously kneaded a paper napkin. I was relieved when Manfred returned with another round of beers. He spoke briefly to Elke in Danish, but she didn't answer him or look in his direction. Instead, she filled her glass again from the new bottle. She took a large gulp of this fresh glass.

She moved even closer to me now, her face so near to mine that I could feel her heat.

"I have to tell you zomthing."

"What?"

"I know a man who wants you."

"Oh? Who?"

"Manfred. Manfred wants you."

"Elke—" Manfred said again in the same understated tone, as if I were not the issue.

"Excuse me?" I said, more confused than shocked as my mind now felt heavy as a battleship and just as cumbersome.

"You must understand," Elke said, ignoring Manfred. "Manfred is not my husband. We live together for three years now. And sometimes, for a while, Margarethe lived with us, too."

Margarethe," I said. I saw my hand raising my bottle again to my lips as I asked Elke, "Why did Margarethe live with you?"

"Because I love Manfred, and I love Margarethe, too," she said in submerged tones.

Margarethe. A hazy picture formed in my mind—Margarethe and Elke, Margarethe and Manfred, Margarethe's disdain for me.

I wobbled with Elke now, my brain wet and sinking. I was waterlogged, too unbalanced to swim. And too drunk to care.

I nodded my head.

"We all love each other, you see. It is very friendly, not jealous. It is very good for me. I get so excited, if I know Manfred is with Margarethe, I have to stop what I am doing and–

"Elke!" Manfred said, stopping her, "our friend doesn't want to know these things."

"Oh, do you not want to know these things?"

"It's all right."

The radiators released a prolonged hissing sound. The boarders were shouting at each other, arguing about something. They had also overdone it. One got up and raised the volume on the TV but the other, the short, puffy one, continued to raise his voice over it.

Manfred remained as impassive as ever. How could he sit there and just say nothing? Elke continued to speak. "Manfred is a very good lover..."

"No, thanks." I avoided Manfred's eyes and downed more beer.

"Elke–" Manfred tried to interrupt her again but Elke ignored him this time.

"Don't be afraid," Elke said. She put her hand over mine. Her palm was hot. It burned the back of my hand, then the burning went up my arm and down my side.

Elke had my hand. We were both drowning now, having been washed overboard in the night, in a deep, tempestuous sea. I went under, struggled to come up, and went under again. Elke had my hand. She would drag me down with her, and this time I wouldn't make it back up.

"Manfred would never hurt you. He is so gentle. I am not jealous. I want to make him happy. I want to be there, too, just to watch, not to say anything. I will sit in a chair. And, of course, I want you, too."

Elke's ponds became larger and deeper. I stared into them as I fell deeper and deeper, drowning in them, drowning in inebriation, drowning in my own oblivion.

"I don't think our friend is of our religion," Manfred said.

He reached over the table and grasped Elke's arm.

"No, she is not of our religion," Elke repeated, giving me a pitying smile.

Manfred's words fished me out of the water.

"No, I'm not," I said, freeing my hand from Elke's hold.

I stood up abruptly, suddenly revived and resuscitated, and with such force that I knocked the chair over, which crashed loudly with the weight of my heavy coat that had been hanging on the back.

"I have to go."

"Don't be afraid," Elke said.

"I'm not afraid," I insisted.

Then I grabbed my coat from the floor, righted the chair and ran out the door without looking back.

My heart pounding, I stumbled down the hallway and fell to my knees once before I got to my door. I had stood up too quickly and my balance was off. Inside my room, I felt even worse as a wave of nausea erupted. I dropped the coat, ran to the bathroom and threw up. I could taste the disgusting combination of the overly rich dinner, the wine and the beer and rinsed my mouth a number of times.

I locked myself in my room. I was shaking and could barely stand up. My head once again felt like a solid block of iron that someone was hammering with a metal mallet. I leaned on the sink, stared at the mirror, at my disheveled face, my eye makeup now smeared and runny. I furiously scrubbed the paint off my face, and for some reason this made me cry. I cried and pulled the barrette out of my hair and frantically brushed it into its normal state, then ripped my clothes off, haphazardly throwing the shoes, the hose, the dress, the slip around the room, letting them land where they may. I quickly changed into wool pants, a warm sweater, and boots. I had to get out of there. This was the only rational thought that emerged from my swirling, shaking, sobbing self.

I washed my face once more, dried my eyes and blew my nose, tried to feel some sense of balance against my reeling state. I shoved money into my pants pocket, retrieved my rumpled coat from the floor and left. I ran down the hall, ran out the glass door, bypassing the elevator, ran down the three flights of stairs and through the front door, where I ran into the perfectly-safe-here Danish night.

Chapter 14

There is nothing more defeating than trying to be sober when you are dead drunk. Two cups of strong black coffee in the first café I found were not the magical antidote that I desired them to be for the poison that I had consumed. I was somewhat improved but still felt enormously heavy, as if my body had hardened into a solid mass. Every step took great effort. I desperately wished to regain my equilibrium, but this eluded me as well as my presence of mind, which was as submersed as a sunken ship. My rescue efforts had been futile; my mind remained buried at sea.

I found myself at Elizabeth's apartment building, but to this day I can't remember going there. I had tried to call her from the café but, of course, there was no answer. I only remember waking up in the back seat of a cab, where I had passed out, with the driver shaking me, saying that we had arrived in Christianshavn. I stood outside the building, disoriented, but I knew where I was and felt relieved to be there.

The night air woke me further. It was brutally cold, and I went inside as much for the warmth as for the hope of finding Elizabeth at home. I didn't consider the unreasonableness of this idea, as there had been no answer when I phoned, but I didn't know what else to do or where else to go. I didn't want to spend another night at Hotel Blumendahl, not when The Two had the key to my room.

I slowly climbed the four flights of stairs to Elizabeth's apartment, using the banister as a crutch the whole way. A hollow, middle-of-the-night silence engulfed the building. I hesitated outside Elizabeth's door, catching my breath. Then I knocked gently three times. No answer. Three more knocks, slightly louder, also received no answer.

"Elizabeth?" I called quietly, standing closer.

I heard nothing. I pressed my ear to the door but again silence.

This time I knocked still louder.

"Elizabeth?"

In spite of the senselessness of my actions, I could not stop knocking and calling out her name.

"Elizabeth? Elizabeth? It's me, Elizabeth?"

It was as if I thought that if I knocked loudly and long enough she would appear. Like an afterthought I heard her name ricocheting into the deep canyon of the stairwell. The whole building must have heard me, but no one emerged to see who was making all the noise.

The thought also occurred to me that I was going to

be stuck here in the depths of Christianshavn. It must have been past 2:00 a.m. Why hadn't I asked that driver to wait?

Weary from the knocking and shouting, I nestled myself against the door, my cheek touching it, and whispered, "Why aren't you home?" to the spirit of Elizabeth.

I reached for the knob in order to rest my hand there, but to my amazement it turned and the door opened.

This startled me more than anything since the entire weight of my body had been pressed against the door and I almost collapsed when it gave way. My grip on the knob saved me from falling–my immediate concern–so that it took me a few seconds to get my bearings, which wasn't hard since the apartment lights were on.

I had my back to the room and when I turned around I gasped loudly at the sight of Elizabeth, who was lying in a disheveled state on the sofa and whose spectral presence had momentarily frightened me. She had caught me so off guard; I never expected her to be there. At first I morbidly feared the worst, but even from across the room I could see her chest rising and falling underneath her blouse.

I just stood there at first, wondering what to do. I had now become an intruder. Perhaps I should have left, but I didn't want to.

Cautiously, I approached her, taking little steps towards her as if I were coming upon an animal in the wild that I wanted to observe at closer range, not wanting to wake her up suddenly and frighten her.

She lay on her right side with one leg dangling over the edge of the couch and the other straight out. Her head had fallen on her right arm, which also extended as if she were reaching for something, and the other was arched in an arabesque above her head. Her hair draped over one cheek, half covering her face. A notebook was spread open on the small coffee table with a pencil lying across it.

"Elizabeth?" I said in a low voice.

I was now next to the table. I knelt down to examine the notebook. The writing was in Danish and looked like a poem in stanzas, but even though I couldn't read the words, I could tell that the writing was erratic; many words had been crossed out with heavy, scribbly lines.

I sat on my knees in front of Elizabeth's face. I thought it would be best if I tried to wake her up. Then I saw the wine bottles, two of them, which were reclining on their sides on the floor between the sofa and the table and a knocked over empty wine glass, as if it, too, had passed out.

"Oh, no," I said aloud, "not you, too." I sighed. "You and I *are* the same girl."

I gently nudged her shoulder.

"Elizabeth?"

She was solidly asleep. The drunkenness lingered on her face like a layer of pancake that she had yet to remove. I brushed the thick hair off her face and tucked it behind her ear. In spite of her state, she still looked sweet and intelligent and beautiful. I missed her eyes, whose intense blue wisdom I needed at that moment. I longed to talk to her.

I hated seeing Elizabeth like that, fragile and pathetic, her body limp and strewn about the couch as if she had been tossed there from across the room. A large wine stain like a gigantic birth mark had spoiled the front of the white blouse, which was now as wrinkled as an old salt's face. I lifted her leg and moved her arm to her front, rearranged her on the sofa so that she lay flatter on her back. She was amazingly heavy for such a slight woman, shrouded in the weight of a drunken sleep.

I so wanted to wake her up. Being with her unconscious like that made me feel even more dreadfully alone. But she clearly needed to sleep this one off, and now that I had discovered her I felt compelled to give her what she needed.

The thought occurred to me that I should try to move her to the bed. I didn't know how I would manage to carry her, limp and heavy as she was now. I was barely able to carry myself, and I was finally beginning to feel very tired.

I sat on the floor and took off my boots. I decided the thing to do would be to leave her where she was and make her comfortable. I turned off the lamp closest to her face and the one overhead and left on the skinny standing brass lamp that hid in the corner by the bookshelves.

I went to the bedroom, where I collected one plump,

feathery pillow and the comforter, and returned to Elizabeth. I gingerly picked up her head and placed the pillow under it. I was about to cover her with the blanket but the large wine stain stopped me. It made her look like she had been bleeding from a deep wound. I also noticed a red mark from the wine that had dried right below her neck.

I left her once more and went to the bathroom. I found a clean washcloth, which I soaked in hot water, and a face towel. Sitting next to her again on the edge of the sofa cushion, I washed her hands, figuring that they might also be sticky from the wine.

They were delicate hands, with small fingers and smooth skin. I loved the way they felt, so soft and small. I could have held them for a long time. I felt a sudden urge to brush my cheek against the back of her right hand after I had dried it with the towel and placed it on her abdomen, but I didn't dare. I wondered if my ablutions would rouse her but she appeared to be no less unconscious than before. I then wiped the stain from her chest. I could see that it also went farther down so I unbuttoned the shirt two more buttons and opened it. As I wiped the last vestige of wine from Elizabeth's upper chest, the edge of my hand brushed the soft round of breast that was spilling out the top of her bra. I quickly pulled my hand away.

I closed the shirt again and covered her up to her chin with the comforter. She looked better to me now, even in her sleep. I had taken a deep pleasure in attending to her and making her clean again, which gave me a clean feeling too.

I decided to stay and sleep in Elizabeth's bedroom. But as soon as I entered the room, I changed my mind, not wanting her to wake up first and discover me. Instead, I took the other pillow and a folded woolen blanket at the foot of the bed and made myself a bedroll on the carpet next to the sofa, where she slept.

I turned off the lamp in the corner. The street lamp threw a wash of light into the room, enough to see without stumbling into the furniture but not enough to keep one awake.

I knelt down to her face and kissed her cheek.

"Good night," I whispered.

Her face shone like a cloudy moon in the darkness and she smelled strongly of wine and that heady floral perfume. I felt an ache deep in my chest. At the time, I did not understand this pain never having felt anything like it before. The more I looked at Elizabeth's beautiful moon glow face, the more I felt this pain until it became unbearable. I began to cry and buried my face in the comforter at her belly, throwing my arms around her cushioned shape. Which was the last thing I remembered...

Shortly after dawn, a diffuse winter light saturated the

room and woke me up. I had slept in the makeshift bedroll curled on my side, and when I raised my head to see the light in the window and the pale somber sky, I felt enormous kinks in my shoulders and back from having camped on the floor. I had to maneuver myself very slowly to get up. Elizabeth was still mercifully asleep. Her head, hooded by the comforter, faced the back of the sofa.

I folded the blanket and returned it and its sister pillow to the bedroom. An inner clock told me that it was time to go. I turned to the next clean page in Elizabeth's writing book and left her a note explaining how I had found the door unlocked and, in a light-hearted manner, admonished her to be more careful about leaving the door open for strangers to wander in, and that I would call her later that morning.

Wrapping myself again in coat, scarf and gloves, I braced myself for the cold, damp Copenhagen morning. I engaged the lock on the door and shut it tightly behind me.

When I was once again in my room, I did not analyze, I did not question, and I did not hesitate. I began to pack.

I was never clearer about any choice in my life than that I needed to leave at once. I decided to go to Zurich for no other reason than the fact that I had consulted the train schedules and discovered a train leaving late that afternoon, and then Switzerland seemed so benign, the land of cuckoo clocks and Heidi chalets tucked into bucolic mountain hillsides.

I packed in a flurry with a single-mindedness that made the whole process speedy. I was anxious to leave without having to see Elke or Manfred, and it was still early enough so that neither of them would yet be up and at their chores. I would be losing two nights' worth of krone, but this was well worth a clean break.

I dropped the wolf book into my handbag, flung it over my shoulder, and opened the door. I looked up and down the hallway. On seeing no one and hearing nothing I breathed a deep sigh of relief. Closing the door very quietly, I brought my suitcase to the desk and parked it by my feet. I picked up a pad of blank paper behind the desk, thinking that I would write them a note, then changed my mind and dropped it again. There was nothing to say. I simply left the key on the desk and reached down to pick up my suitcase.

"You are leaving?"

Elke. Where on earth had she come from? With her unnerving ability to appear suddenly, as if she could walk through walls.

I took a breath and slowly turned around.

Elke stood in the threshold of her door, which was open a thin lightning crack, in bare feet, wearing a flimsy floral bathrobe made of an unnaturally shiny synthetic material. She looked as though she had just woken up and was not at her best. She was even paler than usual with dark half moons under her eyes, which made her seem sickly and evanescent at once. She hugged her arms close to her chest and must have been freezing in such an outfit with bare feet on the cold floors.

"Yes, I am."

"But it is so early."

"So it is."

"You are angry with me. I know you would be angry with me today. You must not be angry."

"I'm not angry," I protested.

"But you are leaving." She gestured at the suitcase by my feet.

"I changed my plans, that's all."

Elke looked warily at me, then smiled.

"Come, I will make coffee," and she pulled her door shut and started walking towards the lounge.

"No! I mean no, thank you, I really have to go."

I picked up my suitcase and, with determination, headed for the glass door but she beat me to it and stood in my way.

"Must you leave?"

"Yes, I must," I said, staring down at the metal clasps on the top of my suitcase.

Elke hugged herself again.

"I have done a terrible thing then. I am very sorry."

Her aqua eyes looked truly remorseful.

"No, you haven't. Don't worry about it. I just can't stay."

"Where will you go so early in the morning? Stay for breakfast and—"

"Elke, please let me by. I have to go."

"Yes, I can see."

She opened the glass door for me one last time and stood there while I waited for the lumbering old lift to arrive.

"Maybe someday you will come again?

"Maybe."

The elevator reached the landing and Elke held the door open with her back so that I could lift my suitcase into it.

"Goodbye," she said, extending her hand.

I shook her cool, dry, soon-to-be-non-existent hand and said "goodbye".

She didn't let go.

"When you remember me, promise you won't hate me?"

"I won't hate you," I promised, giving her a genuine smile.

She let go of my hand and released the elevator. I watched her disappear as the door slid closed on the pretty Scandinavian face with the chilly sea blue eyes.

I knew exactly were I would go: to the train station to check my bag and call Elizabeth. To my amazement and relief and joy she answered and agreed to meet me, she swore this time with her life, at Rådhuspladsen, under the

Town Hall clock in an hour. She could not stop expressing her amazement, confusion and delight with my secret evening at her apartment and couldn't wait to hear more about it.

She wanted me to tell her the story on the phone and when I insisted that I would tell her later she said, "You are a very mysterious girl and so brave again to come in the night."

It was the slowest hour in my life, I couldn't think of an hour that was more excruciatingly slow; every minute seemed like five and every five like fifteen. The walk to Rådhuspladsen would take me no more than ten and the other fifty felt like an unbearable ordeal to endure. I attempted to read the wolf book, but my mind wandered. I left the train station and window shopped, which did not work for passing time in the usual manner since I must have checked my watch every other minute.

By the time I stood waiting under the Town Hall clock ten minutes early, I had wound myself into a Gordian knot. I paced nervously and worried. What if she didn't show up? How long should I wait? What if she didn't show up? Then what would I do? What if she didn't show up? Should I try to call her again? What if she didn't show up? What if she did?

She showed up.

I could see her walking briskly towards me, her hands characteristically confined to her pockets. Then as she saw me she liberated them and waved. I waved back and felt my heart lift. I couldn't stand still, I had to walk towards her. We met halfway and gave each other a long, good-humored, vigorous hug and a few pecks on the cheek.

"How are you?" I asked her, noticing how rested and fresh she looked against all my expectations.

"I am very good, especially to see my friend. Are you hungry?"

"Famished."

"Good. We will eat and you will tell me your great story."

She linked arms with me and informed me that she was taking me to a very good place for breakfast close by and that she was so happy to see me and how disappointed she was that she didn't get to see me last night and apologized for being so rude as to not wake up.

"Oh, no, I must apologize for intruding on you."

"There is no such thing here," she said. "A friend is always a friend. Do you think if I was awake I would not let you in?"

"No, of course not."

"Then why shouldn't you come in when I am asleep?"

"But it's not the same."

"Of course it is the same. You make these things too complicated."

"Perhaps I do."

Over an enormous breakfast of eggs, rolls, smoked fish and rich coffee, I told her the story of Elke and Manfred, which I recounted in gruesome detail. Elizabeth listened attentively but silently, eating and nodding her head and "hmming" at appropriate intervals her eyes widening. But when I got to the part about Manfred saying that I wasn't of their religion she put down her fork and exploded into uncontrollable laughter. She tried to stop and say "not of our religi–pfffff" and erupted into another spasm of belly laughs.

"Just what is so funny?" I asked a little indignantly, feeling that she was laughing at me.

"Oh," she said, regaining her composure and wiping her eyes with a napkin, "this is the funniest story I have heard in a long time. Oh, these Danes. They are too much."

"They certainly are."

"You are right to leave. Where will you go now?"

I told Elizabeth my plans and then we talked about our lives: our immediate futures, our distant futures, what our dreams were and if we thought we would have them.

Then time played its usual trick of being the opposite of what we wanted and hours had passed and it was time to leave.

Elizabeth was headed towards an undisclosed destination on the other side of the city, and she walked me part of the way to the train station until we arrived at a street corner where she said I had to turn and she had to go straight. She took both of my hands in hers and looked into my eyes.

"I have so much liked you. I have much happiness to know you. You will remember me?"

"How could I not remember you? Of course I will."

"We can write. If you would send me some English books, I would like it very much. The women. The poets."

"Absolutely, no question."

"Goodbye, my friend."

She dropped my hands and hugged me close to her, and I hugged her back. "We are the different ones, but we are the same girl, so we will know each other."

It was a moment I wanted never to pass, a connection I wanted never to end. I felt such excruciating joy and such excruciating remorse at the same time. But in a matter of seconds it was over.

Elizabeth let go of me and kissed my cheek.

"Take care," I said.

"And you," she said, waved, turned around and walked along the crowded sidewalk.

I didn't turn. I stood there watching Elizabeth's back as she moved farther and farther away from me and I intermittently lost her and found her again in the moving sea of people.

Then she was gone.

Chapter 15

I sat at the cavernous train station of immense proportions of length, width and height, with still an hour and a half to kill. By this time I was exhausted and much the worse for wear; the previous evening had caught up with me and I looked forward to the long, peaceful train ride. I could do nothing but sit on the worn wooden bench and stare into space. This seemed not an unlikely occupation at the time. I had finally managed to get my brain to stop thinking. I was content to watch the comings and goings of other passengers and to listen to the ethereal female voice that pervaded and echoed throughout the station, announcing arrivals and departures in Danish and in English. I had collected my suitcase, which now lay by my feet like a faithful pet. Emptied of emotion and, lost in that egoless state, time was finally kind to me and passed quickly and the moment arrived for my stay in Copenhagen to become a memory.

I remained true to my vow to Elizabeth, for whom there will always be a place in my heart. Elizabeth grew more beautiful through the years, and more loving and wise and never aged. But for some reason, which still eludes me, I neglected to write to her or send her the books that she had asked for, feeling guilty about this for years. And I often wondered what would have happened if we had kept in touch. My wish for Elizabeth was that she found her happiness again and that she wrote ever more beautiful poems. I have never met anyone else like her, and I will never forget her.

As for Olaf I could only remember him fondly as well. I hoped that he finally found his soulmate and that he had a flock of bouncy, adorable children.

I was also true to my promise to Elke, whom I did not hate but treated like the exotic hothouse flower that she was and grew to understand her more and more as the years passed. I told the story of Elke and Manfred often, sometimes with a few embellishments here and there, a great party pleaser or in more intimate moments, to impress a new lover in the early months of our relationship with the range of my experience, though, surely by that time, I had already made an adequate impression.

But until now—which suddenly strikes me as peculiar—I have never told anyone this story, this truth that I have kept secret within me like a treasure lost deep beneath the seas: how the strange bird-like woman led me to the harbor that day, much against my will, and how I found and how, when I thought no one was looking, I touched the metal girl.